The Mother Tree

RUTH WHITEHEAD

The Mother Tree

drawings by Charles Robinson

THE SEABURY PRESS

NEW YORK

For My Mother

Contents

The Mother Tree

CHAPTER 1

✽

Explorers All

WHO WOULD VENTURE AMONG CATCLAW BUSHES and thorny agarita to find a last year's bird's nest? Tempe Foster would, for she was a collector. Who would go out on a summer afternoon under the blazing Texas sun to pick up rocks, pincushion cactus, arrowheads (a rare find), and interesting looking bones? Tempe would, and so would Opal, her best friend.

Tempe and Opal had been exploring since noon and carried sacks, heavy with loot, slung over their shoulders. With them was Tempe's little sister, Laurie. The three girls, wearing long-waisted dresses and calico sunbonnets, with Tempe in the lead, plodded along the rocky path. All were hot and thirsty. Laurie, dragging her rag doll, was hot and thirsty and tired and cross. Four years old, she was rather young for exploring.

"Temp-ee," Laurie wailed, falling far behind. "Carry me!"

"Just a little way," encouraged Tempe, with her eyes on the shady spot ahead, "and we'll be at the creek."

Laurie gave up suddenly, sat down in the dirt and began to cry.

"Oh, my goodness," said Tempe. She and Opal held Laurie's hands, and the three hurried toward the inviting deep shade of the pecan trees.

It was heavenly along the creek. Cool, clear water gurgled over stones into a shallow pool. The girls dipped water with their hands and drank, then collapsed on a grassy slope, took off their bonnets and fanned their warm faces. A south breeze rustled the leaves high overhead, birds twittered, and grasshoppers made giant leaps in the Johnson grass.

Laurie, the loudest complainer, was the first to recover. In a few minutes she was talking to her doll about grasshoppers. Though the doll said nothing, Laurie scrambled to her feet and announced, "Butterflake wants me to catch a grasshopper."

"Good," said Tempe lazily, "you do that."

Laurie asked the girls, "Want me to catch you some?"

Winking at Opal, Tempe replied, "Catch six of them. That'll keep you busy until time to go home."

Opal grinned. "Three for me, three for Tempe."

The best thing about Opal was her patience with Laurie. Only a best friend would always accept a tag-a-long little sister.

Laurie chased grasshoppers in the weeds. Tempe rose and picked up her sack. She asked Opal, "Want to see what we've got?"

"Yes."

They poured their treasures on the ground, sat cross-legged, and began looking them over. Almost every week the girls planned to be together. The visits were at Tempe's house, or at Opal's, or at a halfway meeting place. It was lonesome in the country during the long summer vacation, with no chance to see school friends except on Sundays at the crossroads church. Tempe felt lucky that Opal lived only two miles away, near enough for walking visits. —

Tempe and Opal had been friends since first grade; now they were almost eleven. It was easy to be friends, two girls with like ideas, sharing a double desk at school. Both were collectors; both believed in dividing treasures half and half. Opal wasn't bossy and didn't try to change Tempe's mind. Tempe tried to be the same with Opal.

The girls were not much alike, really. Tempe bounced about on slim legs with her brown braids flying, but sometimes she wore a worried look. Opal had a round, happy face and giggled a lot. When Tempe worried about Laurie, or was mad at her big brother, Philip, Opal's good nature cheered her.

Because Tempe climbed every tree in sight, Opal thought she was brave. Opal, who recited poems and could spell "Biloxi, Mississippi" without catching her breath, was a clever girl, Tempe said, a clever genius. Opal could reel off names and dates of all the twenty-six Presidents, every single one of them, from George Washington right down to Theodore Roosevelt, who was in the White House now.

In school, Tempe and her deskmate helped each other with long division and puzzling verbs like "go, went, gone." They were partners. And collecting was their greatest joy. If they couldn't find a fossil, a rock that looked like a fossil was good to keep. If they couldn't catch a redbird (and who could?), a brilliant tail feather was almost the same. And an arrowhead, what a prize! They pounced on that. It was good for trading. Boys, even, drooled over arrowheads. Boys had been known to trade agates and real gold rings for arrowheads.

Today they had found rocks that looked like granite, cactus that looked like toadstools, and a bone that Opal said was a dinosaur's elbow.

"Are you sure they had elbows?" asked Tempe.

"Sure I'm sure," said Opal, and that settled it. Tempe did not agree, but you don't dispute the word of your best friend. The bone went into Opal's collection.

When the shade of the pecan tree grew long Tempe tried not to notice that the day was going fast. Opal could stay until sundown, but not she. Opal had a mother who cooked supper, and she had no little sister following her about, asking her questions, taking up her time. Tempe sighed. It wasn't fair . . .

Sorting rocks, she thought to herself: I won't turn around and find how low the sun is, I won't look. But when the shadow of the pecan stretched clear across the creek, Tempe squinted her eyes almost shut and looked to the west. She sighed again. _

"It's getting along toward suppertime," she said, putting away her treasures. "Time to go."

"So early?" Opal wrinkled her nose and frowned.

"I have to round up Laurie and head home." Tempe picked up her tow sack and looked around. "Laurie!" she called.

A squeaky voice came from down the creek. "Come get me."

Tempe rolled her eyes. "You come to me!" she shouted.

The squeaky voice said, "No, no, no!"

Opal giggled. Tempe began to walk away. "Good-bye, Laurie. We're going . . ."

"Temp-ee—" The voice was begging now.

"If you hurry, we'll wait."

Tall weeds rustled, and the calico bonnet came in sight. A sing-song voice began, "Tempe's mean, let's both scream, Tempe's mean, going to tell Father—"

"Who's she talking to?" asked Opal.

Tempe rolled her eyes again. "Who knows? Her pet tiger, her pooka—"

"Pooka?"

"That's an animal Granny told her about. Laurie has a lot of pets, in her mind."

Laurie galloped out of the weeds riding a crooked stick, dodged Tempe's outstretched hand and disappeared in the other direction.

"Laurie!" Tempe lost patience. "If you don't come this minute—"

Laurie circled and came back, laughing with glee. "Tempe's a skunk, and she gets drunk—"

Opal gasped.

Tempe muttered, "Wait till I get my hands on that Phil! He taught her that." She wanted to say Philip was himself a skunk, but something held her tongue. Family pride, maybe. As Granny often said, "The Foster family has to stick together." To herself Tempe wondered, did sticking together mean putting up with a sassy big brother who thought he knew as much as Father?

Tempe dropped her sack, ran after Laurie and led her back to the clearing. She knelt and pulled Laurie, warm and squirming, into the circle of her arms. "Untied, un-buttoned," she grumbled, as her strong hands tied shoe-laces and put Laurie's clothes in order. "Bonnet strings tangled." Laurie scowled but did not resist. When Tempe gave her a loving spank and released her, she bounced along the path.

Opal handed Laurie her crooked stick. "Here's your pony."

"It's not a pony," said Laurie. "It's my pooka." She climbed astride the stick and galloped ahead.

Opal asked, as they strolled along, "Do you ever get tired of taking care of Laurie?"

"Well," Tempe began, "I'm used to it, ever since

8

Mother—" Her voice stumbled, trying to explain, then dwindled. She tried to remember what it had been like, before she took charge of Laurie. Only last winter, she thought, when Laurie was three, it had been Mother who brushed Laurie's tangled hair, undressed her and rocked her to sleep. It seemed like a long time ago. "Well," Tempe began again, "she's little, and she depends on me."

"My brothers don't depend on me. We all depend on Mama."

"We did, too. Now it's Father."

"Do you ever cry when you think about your mother?"

"At first I did." Tempe remembered the empty rocking chair and the wind blowing down the stovepipe in the night—wind that sounded like Mother's voice, calling. "At first we all cried and couldn't talk about it, but Laurie asked so many questions—"

"Questions?"

"We've explained so many times to Laurie, I guess we've got over crying."

"Explained about your mother?"

"Yes." Tempe stopped walking, for they had come to the fork of the country lane. She and Laurie would go south, Opal north. "Over and over, she asks when Mother is coming home."

Opal's eyes were almost frightened. "She does? But doesn't she know?"

"Laurie believes what she feels," said Tempe, "not

9

what she knows. She wants Mother home, so she believes she will be back."

Opal stared. "Really?"

"Father says she's too young to know the difference between feeling and knowing. He says we should be patient with her until she's older."

"My goodness," said Opal soberly.

Tempe glanced at the sun; it was sliding fast. "Good-bye, Opal. See you next week?"

"I'll meet you," promised Opal, "same place. Bye."

Tempe called to Laurie, who was prancing in circles, and swung down the lane toward home. Laurie stopped prancing and trudged along beside her. Another mile, and they would be home. Tempe dreaded this stretch of the road. It was hard to be brave, walking here. It made her think of last winter, and of the fever, quick and cruel.

One week Mother rocked and sang, "Green Grows the Laurel"; the next week she moaned with a fever. When the fever rose up and up, Mother's voice and the song were swept away.

"Your mother had pneumonia," Father told her, "and sometimes it is quick and cruel."

Tempe understood it with her mind but not with her heart. But today she had to think of something else. She had to think of something to keep Laurie's mind busy when they passed the graveyard. She heard the threshing of wings overhead and saw a black crow flap into the gnarled mesquite tree beside the road. "Look, Laurie," she said, "a crow."

There was no answer from under Laurie's sunbonnet. They tramped along. The fence of the graveyard was just ahead. Tempe tried to brighten her voice. "I know a story . . ." Laurie said nothing. "Once there was this animal, half horse and half billy goat. He had horns, and when he opened his mouth you never knew if he would whinny like a horse or bleat like a goat, or talk out loud." Laurie put her hand in Tempe's. "Do you know what his name was?" Laurie did not answer. "The old folks called him 'pooka.' "

Under the bonnet there was silence. Tempe stepped at a brisker pace. They were almost past the graveyard. Again the flutter of crow's wings was overhead. A raucous "caw-caw" shattered the stillness of the countryside as the crow roared away against the sky.

Startled by the noise, Laurie pulled her hand free, then clutched Tempe's fingers again. Her voice came, slow and firm. "Tem-pe . . ."

"Yes?"

"When will Mother be home again?"

Tempe dropped Laurie's hand. Her feet slowed; her heart dragged. She couldn't outsmart Laurie's feelings. She wondered how a little girl could have such a long memory.

Tempe, too, had a long memory. She remembered happier times at home, two and three years before. Now things were different and she knew it; there was only Father to tuck them under the covers at night.

Tempe, who was almost eleven years old, and brave most of the time, knew what had happened and believed what had happened. Laurie, who was only four, could not believe it.

Father's words came to Tempe. "Give Laurie time. Be patient."

Tempe did not scold. The dull ache that came from remembering wouldn't let her say anything. Finally she knelt and put her arms around Laurie.

"Mother is in the graveyard," said Tempe. "She can't come home again."

CHAPTER 2

❧

She Depends on Me

AT HOME, TEMPE SPREAD HER ROCKS and cactus on the back porch. To keep them safe from everybody's feet, she put them on the floor below the shelf that held her precious arrowheads. The redbird feather decorated the wall calendar in the kitchen, pinned to the picture of Little Liver Pills.

She poured water in the wash pan and helped Laurie wash her hands and face. Father and Philip, who were threshing grain at a neighbor's farm three miles away, would be home at sundown. Everyone would be hungry, especially Phil, who could eat twice as much as anybody else, and eat it twice as fast.

At Tempe's loud complaints about Phil's appetite, Father said, "When a boy is fourteen, his stomach is a bottomless pit."

The words made Laurie laugh aloud. "Bottamus pit!" she echoed, pointing one plump finger at her brother. "Bottamus pit, Phil!"

"Humph!" Tempe grunted. What was funny about that? Laurie laughed at the queerest things. And what was funny about a loudmouthed, long-legged boy who came swaggering home, telling his sisters what to do? Phil thought he was a man now, working on the grain thresher crew. Tempe knew better. He was only an errand boy. Among the men, no doubt Phil said, "Yes sir, no sir—right away, sir." How she would love to hear that! She'd like to be there when the men yelled, "Water boy!" and see him jump. The image was so strong and so tantalizing, Tempe had trouble pulling her mind back to the kitchen.

Boil the beans and sweep the floor and make the beds, she had reminded herself that morning before she left the house. Boil the beans early like Father said, so they'll be tender. She lifted the heavy lid of the kettle. Pinto beans and ham hocks floated in rich red-brown gravy. They were just right. The delicious smell made her stomach growl with hunger. The family would have lettuce and tomatoes from the garden, too, and hot corn bread and glasses of milk.

She needed eggs to stir into the corn bread batter. None were in the kitchen cupboard. "Laurie," she called, "want to go with me to gather eggs?" Laurie skipped ahead of Tempe on the worn path to the chicken pen. "Easy now, don't make them flutter."

Laurie tiptoed to the gate and put her face against the wire netting. "Howdy, hens, howdy, eggs," she began in a sing-song voice.

Tempe eased through the gate and moved toward the

laying boxes, chattering to soothe the chickens. Some came running for food, others went on pecking at the ground, scratching and clucking. The first nest was empty, and so were the second and third. The fourth nest, as she had expected, was crowded with brown eggs.

"That's right, ladies," Tempe told the hens, "plenty of nests and what do you do? You all pile into one!" She put the eggs carefully into her sunbonnet and held it in the crook of her arm. "Thank you for the eggs!" The hens sang and scratched.

Laurie peeked through the wire gate. "I want to scratch the pig."

Tempe wanted to hurry back to the kitchen, but no, Laurie must visit the animals, her daily routine. Tempe found a bucket to hold the bonnetful of eggs and set it by the gate. Peter the pig rushed to the fence to meet them. Nothing frightened the pig, and empty-handed visitors disgusted him. He oinked loudly for food. "Sorry, Peter," Tempe told him, "we'll feed you the scraps after supper."

After supper didn't mean anything to Peter. He was hungry right now. His oinks didn't let up until Laurie stuck the old barn broom through the fence rails and scratched his back. The broom was too big for Laurie to handle. One stroke in three touched Peter's back, but the attention soothed him. He settled down to contented grunts.

Tempe took Laurie's hand. "Let's go." There was a

lot to do in the kitchen before the men got home.

"No!" Laurie pulled away. "I want to talk to Molly."

Tempe was annoyed. The sun was almost down. She had to bring in wood and get the stove hot. She patted her foot and frowned. "Oh, all right. But hurry!"

The cow was at the pasture gate, home for supper and for milking. Laurie climbed halfway up the gate, patted the soft folds on Molly's neck and began her sing-song. "Molly, Molly, you're so soft, soft and warm, like a lolly." Nobody knew what a lolly was; Laurie liked rhymes. Cranky old Molly, who wouldn't let anyone touch her outside the milking stall, fell under the spell of the chanting voice. She chewed her cud, and with only a flick of an ear, let Laurie stroke her.

Back in the kitchen Tempe stoked the fire and mixed corn bread batter the way Father had taught her, with meal, salt, eggs, and milk. She greased the heavy iron skillet and let it get piping hot. She was about to pour the batter into the skillet when an uneasy thought struck her.

She flew to the cupboard and stared anxiously at the supplies. Flour, sugar, coffee, cinnamon, pepper-sauce, baking powder—that was it, baking powder to make the bread rise.

A feeling of relief made her weak. That other time she had forgotten both baking powder and salt. The bread had turned out flat, hard, and tasteless. Philip had taken one bite and brayed like a donkey. Chewing, he had pretended to break off a tooth; Tempe had burst into tears, and Father had scolded.

Now Tempe stirred in the magic white powder, happy that she had remembered. The batter sizzled when she poured it in the skillet and began to get light and puffy. Halfway back on the stove the corn pone would brown on one side. Tempe dreaded the task of turning it over with the flapjack turner. That was the hardest part, and the trickiest. To handle the half-cooked pone, which was the size of a dinner plate, she always stood on a stool. She had to be quick, or the pone would break and spill all over the top of the stove. Father could toss the corn pone over as easy as you please. She hoped he would get home tonight in time to do the turning.

"Laurie," she called, "go outside and see if the wagon is coming."

Laurie tore outside and came right back, slamming the screen door. "No, no, no," she reported, and flew back out again. Two minutes later she was back. "No, no, no!" she shouted and ran out again.

In and out she ran until Tempe said firmly, "All right. Now stop it!"

When it was almost dark they heard the clop of horses' feet and the rattle of the wagon. "Whoa!" came Father's deep voice, and out flew Laurie.

Philip said, "Up she goes!" and her chirping voice turned to shrieks. He carried Laurie on his shoulders and set her down on the steps. Philip was good to Laurie,

Tempe thought. Maybe he wasn't such a bad brother; she would try to hold her temper tonight.

She was standing on the stool with flapjack turner in hand, staring anxiously at the corn pone, wondering if it was time to turn, when Philip's big feet tramped into the kitchen.

"What's for supper?" he asked loudly.

Tempe, teeth clenched, counted to ten. She didn't want him in the kitchen, bothering her. "I'm busy," she told him sharply. "Please leave."

Philip's face didn't change. His big hands raised the kettle's lid; his long neck stretched as he peered inside. The lid fell back with a clatter. "Beans, beans! Can't you cook anything but beans?"

Tempe swung at him with the flapjack turner and missed. "Out, get out! I wouldn't feed you bread and water!"

Philip laughed uproariously. In a high voice he mimicked, "Wouldn't feed you bread and water!" He washed up on the porch, slamming the pan on the table and honking his nose and throat to rid them of the grain chaff. When his feet bumped into Tempe's rock collection she rushed out of the kitchen.

"Oh, can't you ever look where you walk? You've ruined my specimens!"

Philip's smile was a smirk. With one big hand held behind him, and the other poised daintily in the air, he bowed from the waist. "*Beg* your pardon." His voice was

sarcastic. "Your specimens." Then he straightened, and his voice became his own. "Looks like a bunch of trash to me. Why don't you keep 'em at the barn?"

Tempe tried to hit him. When he side-stepped neatly her fist knocked the arrowheads from the shelf and scattered them. Hot tears sprang to her eyes. She stooped to pick up her treasures. "Mean—mean—no supper for you!"

"Says who? I worked hard today. Now I eat."

He had won that point, Tempe thought bitterly. Nobody at the Fosters' ever went to bed hungry, no matter how mean they were. Crouching on the floor, gathering arrowheads into a fold of her apron, she tried to sniff away her tears. Philip could at least help her pick them up, she thought, but no—he was too important. She'd like to see *him* try to put a meal on the table.

Philip stood behind her, with a puzzled frown on his face. He reached out a hand, then drew it back. "Aw, Temp—"

But Tempe wasn't listening. Then the worst thing happened. The very worst. While she crouched on the floor, unable to fight back, Philip reached down and pulled her hair braid.

She leaped to her feet, spilling arrowheads all over the porch, and burst into loud sobs.

"I hate you! I won't cook tomorrow!" she told him. "Won't be here tomorrow. I'll leave home and live at Opal's house. No mean bully boy at Opal's!"

Tempe had forgotten supper. She had forgotten Father and Laurie, until she caught sight of a frightened face peering around a corner of the porch—a small face with big eyes and trembling mouth.

Tempe ran into the kitchen. She climbed on the stool and turned the corn pone. For once, it flopped over, just right. She dished up the supper, slammed the chairs to the table and charged out the door. On the steps she met Father. A surprised look came over his grimy, sweat-stained face. She stopped long enough to gabble, "Supper's ready, hot corn bread. Don't wait for me. Won't sit down at the table with Philip!"

"Now, now," said Father.

She ran to the elm tree and climbed to a spot twice as high as her head. She heard the bump of chairs in the kitchen and the rattle of dishes. She heard Laurie's whining voice. After her heart had stopped thumping she began to feel hungry. Her legs felt numb from crouching in the tree, but she wasn't going to come down, not until Philip said he was sorry. She moved to the tree fork, leaned back and closed her eyes. When she opened them she saw Father standing below.

"I know how you feel, Tempe."

She sobbed, just a little. "I take care of the house all day, then *he* ruins everything!"

"You do a good job," he told her, "but Phil works hard, too. He's on the run all day long, gets covered with that itchy chaff from the grain . . ."

22

Tempe said nothing, gazing down at Father—what she could see of him in the dusk. He had washed up and combed his hair, hair that was growing thin along the top of his head.

"It's important for us all to work together"—Father's voice stopped, and he had to clear his throat before going on—"to lighten the load, since your mother is gone."

Tempe was silent until she heard a wail from the house. Laurie wasn't whining now; she was really crying. "What's the matter with her?"

"She heard you say you'd leave home."

His words struck Tempe like a blow to her stomach. She felt sick.

"Laurie won't eat until you come to the table."

Tempe sat up straight. She was angry again. "Let Philip feed her and talk to her."

"Now, Tempe—"

"That'll teach him it's not easy to do everything!"

Father was silent for a long moment, then asked, "Do you think that will satisfy Laurie?"

Tempe's mouth trembled for a long time before she found her voice. "I—I guess not. She depends on me."

"That's right," said Father.

Tempe looked away and drew a long breath. Why did everybody have to depend on her? It kept her angry half the time, and scared. But she couldn't tell Father that.

"Could . . ." she hesitated, "could you talk to

Laurie?"

"I've tried," he said.

Suddenly Tempe saw there was only one thing to do. She crawled down from the tree fork. Three minutes later she was spooning beans into Laurie's mouth. "One bite for you, and one for me."

The pinto beans and the buttery corn bread were delicious. And it was good to see Father's slow smile as he said, "It's a brave girl who can change her mind."

CHAPTER 3

✿

Wash Day, Work-a-Day

TEMPE WOKE TO A BUSY FARM. Only a dim peach-colored light showed in the east, but sounds told her that Father and Philip were astir. The iron kettle clanged on the kitchen range; Father was cooking breakfast. Philip's ax pounded the chopping block, and at the barnyard Molly bawled for her calf.

Tempe drew away from Laurie, who, with her doll, sprawled over much of the bed. Pulling the quilt under her chin, she closed her eyes for one more nap.

Their double bed was in a corner of the sitting room, the middle room of the house. The kitchen on the north was for cooking and eating. The south room was where Father slept, and also Philip, part of the time. Phil liked to set his cot in a cool spot for summer and in a warm one for winter. His favorite corner when north winds howled was in the attic, beside the warm chimney.

More than anything else Tempe wanted a bedroom. In her mind was a long list of wishes, and if she ever wrote them down they would fill a page of her school tablet. The list would begin, "Number One—bedroom of my own."

Father knew this. He said, "My children are getting as big as yearling calves. This old house is too small. If crops are good this year, I'm going to build a lean-to, then we'll have plenty of room."

Tempe gloated over the thought. Plenty of room! Room for their dresses and Laurie's dolls, and room for Tempe's arrowheads and rocks. A room with a door she could shut. People would have to knock and wait to be invited in.

Father, who understood that Tempe and Laurie needed privacy, had strung a curtain in the corner to hide their bed. In the winter it worked fine. The girls went to bed early while Father and Philip sat by the fireplace with the lamp burning. But now it was summertime, and in hot weather nobody could sleep behind a curtain. Every stray breeze was welcome. All summer long, except on rainy days, the doors and windows stood wide open.

Tempe heard Philip's boots tramp noisily through the sitting room into the bedroom and back again. Why did he have to come through here? she thought resentfully. He could enter his room from the porch. And a thoughtful boy would tiptoe.

The tramping boots were at the foot of her bed. "Get up, sleepyheads!" his voice boomed.

Tempe pulled the quilt tighter and closed her eyes. "Go away, please," she murmured.

Philip only laughed. "Up, before I drag you out!"

Tempe opened her eyes and scowled at him. "You're not my boss."

He laughed again and tugged at the covers. "Up, up!"

Laurie opened her eyes, yawned and stretched. Tempe sat up suddenly with her hair awry and wrapped the quilt closer. "No respect for a girl's privacy—get out!"

That brought a guffaw from Philip; he bent double with it. In a prissy girl's voice he mocked, "No respect for a girl's privacy!"

Tempe hated him all over again. When he pulled the quilt from the bed exposing her naked arms and legs, she threw a pillow at him angrily. He ducked and bellowed, slapping his leg. Laurie gurgled with laughter, but Tempe was ready to cry.

Father's mild voice came from the kitchen. "Stop teasing, Phil. Make haste, girls, put on your clothes. By sunup, your granny and grandpa will be here."

Teasing! How could Father call it teasing? It was torture, Tempe fumed, that's what it was, pure torture.

Laurie bounced out of bed and ran to the window to watch for Grandpa's wagon. Tempe brooded, trying to console herself. She would get even with that devil Philip. Sometime today, she would get him for sure. She began looking for a clean pair of drawers and a dress for Laurie.

As good smells came from the kitchen the girls washed up. Tempe brushed Laurie's hair, buttoned her dress and tied a bow in the back. Then she brushed her own hair.

Her hands hadn't yet learned the knack of making braids in a hurry, so she parted her hair in the middle, pulled half of it to the left side of her head and tied it with a ribbon. When she had done the other side in the same way she was ready for breakfast.

At the table Tempe sat beside Laurie, handy for cutting her food to bite size, for buttering her biscuits, even for spoon-feeding when Laurie could talk her into it.

Philip's chair thumped and bumped when he sat down. Laurie grabbed a biscuit, but at Father's frown, put it back on the plate and ducked her head. Full daylight had crept into the room. Father blew out the pale flicker of the coal-oil lamp, clasped his hands, and bowed his head. "Thank you, Lord. Bless us all." Plates and spoons clattered.

Every day during the past week Father and Philip had left the house by sunup and had come home after dark. The thresher crew worked without letup to harvest the grain while the weather was sunny. Late on Friday night the threshing job had ended. Now it was Saturday; Father and Philip would stay at home, and it would be wash day for the Fosters—for the family here and for Granny and Grandpa who lived two miles down the road.

After breakfast Father said, "Everybody knows what to do on wash day."

Laurie chanted, "Wash day, work-a-day," and once more looked out the window. No wagon was in sight. "Granny and Grandpa day!"

While Father cleared the table, Tempe strained the milk. Laurie wanted to help. "No," said Tempe, "you would spill it."

Laurie's face clouded. She ran outside. Tempe heard her beg Philip, who was filling the washpots with water, to let her pull the rope that hauled the bucket from the well. She liked to hear the pulley squeak. When Philip said, "No, no," Laurie yelled, "Yes, yes!" She wanted to strike the match and light the fire under the washpot. "No," said Philip, "you're too little."

Laurie's voice broke into an angry sob. Tempe heard running steps on the porch and the slam of the screen door as she stormed into the house. "I'm *not* too little!"

Tempe said, "Help me sort the clothes," and pointed to growing heaps on the floor. "Overalls here, underwear there." It was a dreary, endless job, and Tempe hated it. Laurie made a stack of work shirts and overalls that grew and grew until it was higher than her head. Busy, she did not hear the first clip-clop of horses' feet. "Granny's here," Tempe told her and they both ran outside.

Harnesses jangled, and wagon axles groaned. Grandpa braced his feet and pulled mightily on the reins. "Whoa, team!"

The wagon stopped. Granny didn't have to climb down over the front wheel. Father, who was tall like Grandpa, simply reached up, took her off the spring seat and set her on the ground. The sight of Granny flying through the air in Father's arms never failed to excite

Laurie. "Do it again," she begged Father. "Granny's little! Do it again."

Granny *was* little, not much taller than Tempe. Her face was alight. "Laurie girl, Tempe!" She held out her arms, and Laurie ran into them. Tempe wasn't far behind. Granny smelled sweet like talcum powder and clean like homemade soap.

Laurie asked suddenly, "I'm *not* too little, am I?"

"Too little?" Granny blinked her eyes in surprise, but asked no questions. She said firmly, with her chin stuck out, "Of course you're not. Nobody's too little!" Laurie beamed.

Grandpa hugged the girls, then with Philip's help unhitched the horses and put them out to graze. The men unloaded baskets of clothes from the wagon while Tempe and Laurie led Granny into the house.

Granny lost no time in getting to work. She took off her calico bonnet, tied a pink ruffled apron around her waist and began to sort clothes. "Who's the fastest worker in this room?" she asked in a brisk voice, winking at Tempe.

Laurie bragged that she was, and Tempe was absolutely sure that *she* was, but Granny's quick hands made the highest stack of all. Hands flew, and suddenly there were no more clothes to sort; the dismal job had ended. Tempe was astonished; with Granny in charge, the work had melted away.

The sun came up. Hurry, hurry, Granny said, or they

would all go limp in midday heat. Washing was always a race between the Fosters and the summer sun. If they put the clothes on the lines before the fiery old monster had crept past the top of the elm tree, they would win.

Washtubs were set up on the back porch, two for rubbing clothes and two for rinsing. Father and Philip were first at the rub boards. Tempe and Granny kept the fires going and brought hot water. Thump, thump, and splash —the sheets were clean. Rub, rub, went the towels, the underwear, and calico dresses. Next came the grimy shirts and overalls.

When Philip ran out of breath Granny said, "It's my turn now."

Father set a rocking chair on the porch. "You're too little."

Granny scowled up at him. "Out of my way! I may be a granny woman, but I can outwork you younguns!" She winked at the girls and made the soap suds fly. But Granny soon grew tired, so Tempe took her place at the rub board.

The galloping sun grew hot on Tempe's back; sweat plastered her dress to her skin. She looked across at Granny in the rocker with Laurie cuddled beside her.

"Granny," she said, "remember us a song."

"Do you want 'Married Me a Wife'?"

It was an old one from Granny's young days way back in the mountains, and it suited the wash day chore. It went well with the rub-a-dub of the washing. Philip

shouted, "Line it for us, Granny!"

Granny sang the first line,

> "*Married me a wife in the month of June.*"

The family chorus was,

> "*Rissolty, rassolty, row, row, row!*"

Granny wailed,

> "*Carried her home in the light of the moon.*"

Philip and Father and Grandpa boomed,

> "*Hey gee wality, nickety-nollity*
> *Rest of your quality*
> *Nickety, nackety, now, now, now!*"

There were twelve-teen verses, the ones Granny sang and those Tempe and Philip made up as they went along.

> "*She sweeps the floor but once a year*
> *She says that brooms are all too dear.*
>
> *She combs her hair but once a week*
> *She says that combs are all too cheap.*"

The Fosters were red in the face from scrubbing and singing, but the clothes had been rubbed, boiled white, rinsed in blue water, and were ready to hang. The wash was finished, and the sun was only a quarter high. They had won the race with Old Monster Sun.

Father gave Laurie a basketful of socks. It was her task to hang them on a bramble bush to dry. Granny rose from the rocking chair. Her long skirt swished as she led the way to the clotheslines.

"I'll lay the song book on the shelf
If you want any more you can sing it yourself!"

Everybody in the family howled,

"Nickety, nackety, now, now, now!"

CHAPTER 4

❧

Dandelion Will Tell

AFTER THE SUN MOVED TO THE WEST the family gathered on the shady back porch. By now dinner was over and the clothes were dry. Tempe hoped that Father would forget to put the sad irons on the range to heat. He did not forget. Nobody wanted to iron in the hot kitchen, so Father and Philip moved the kitchen table to the porch and padded it to make a wide ironing board. Everybody except Grandpa and Laurie took a turn at ironing.

Philip was mortified at doing what he called "girl's work," but Father did not excuse him. Philip scowled at Tempe. "I won't do your dresses!"

Tempe scowled right back. "Then I won't iron your shirts. So there!"

"You'll each do your own," said Father.

Grandpa shook his head. "Pig-headed younguns!" He asked the family, "Any shoes need a half sole?" Indeed they did, four pairs needed mending. Grandpa went to the wagon and brought back sole-leather, tacks, hammer, and awl. Laurie proudly carried the knee-high last that would hold the shoe while Grandpa mended. Grandpa's silvery head bent over his work as he cut, fitted, and hammered. Tempe and Laurie stood very still, watching him. He was clever with the knife; after tracing a pattern for the new sole he sliced the tough cowhide leather as neatly as Father sliced bacon.

Laurie grew tired of watching and moved to the edge of the porch, sat down and dangled her feet. When Tempe sat down, Laurie leaned against her. Laurie's soft body was warm, too warm. "Move over," said Tempe.

Laurie wouldn't move. "Tell me that story."

Tempe, after hours of rub-a-dub and hot ironing, was sleepy. "What story?" she asked in a lazy voice.

"In your schoolbook."

Tempe lay back on the bare boards of the porch and closed her eyes. "Lots of stories—which one?"

"About the shoemaker and the Little Folks."

"Elves," murmured Tempe, "shoemaker and the elves." She couldn't remember how the story went, she just couldn't. "Take a nap, Laurie."

Laurie fidgeted. Her elbow dug into Tempe's ribs. "Puh-lease," she begged. Tempe opened her eyes to see dangling hair and a face above her own, magnified in size, with pink mouth about to drool.

"I'm tired and sleepy," Tempe told her. "Can't you settle down?"

Laurie scrambled to her feet and asked Grandpa, "Will you whittle me an elf—a little bitty elf?"

Grandpa was a first-class whittler, but today his bushy

36

eyebrows came together in a frown. He grunted, "Foolishness! Can't you see I'm busy?"

"Ask him later," said Granny. She crooked a bony finger at Laurie. "Come to me." Laurie shook her head and begged Philip to let her iron.

"No," said Philip, "you'd drop the iron."

Laurie jumped up and down. "I won't drop the iron," she sputtered, "and I'm *not* too little!"

Father shook his head. "Now, now . . ."

Tempe sat up, drowsy and dizzy. "You're cross, Laurie. Come here and take a nap."

"No," said Laurie, half-crying. "I'm *not* cross!"

Granny was mending overalls. "I do declare, Laurie, we forgot the socks." Laurie turned to listen. "There's always socks for me to darn. Where are they?"

"Hanging on the bramble bush."

"You and Tempe take a basket and bring them to me."

Laurie made a face at Tempe. "Tempe's a skunk," she chanted, "and she gets drunk—"

Philip burst into a loud chortle and almost dropped the iron. Tempe roused, angry all over again. Father shook his head at Laurie. "Now where did you hear that?"

"Tempe won't tell me that story. I'll go by myself!" Laurie flounced off the porch and disappeared around a corner of the house.

Tempe fumed to herself about Philip and his rude horselaugh. It was maddening. Remembering her vow of this morning, she wondered how she could make him sorry. No ideas came, and she drifted into sleep. Some time later when Granny asked, "Where's Laurie? She's been gone a long time," Tempe sat up and yawned.

"Chasing a butterfly, maybe," she grunted, getting to her feet, "or looking for doodlebugs in the dirt." After the short nap Tempe felt refreshed. A breeze had sprung up, cooling her armpits and the moist places behind her knees. "Laurie!" she called, circling the house. "Where *are* you?"

As she had guessed, Laurie was sprawled on the ground. Tempe sang the old song that had Laurel's name in it,

> *"Green grows the laurel*
> *All sparkling with dew*
> *I'm lonely my darling*
> *Since parting with you."*

As Tempe drew near, Laurie didn't look up. She lay on her stomach, with the empty basket beside her. In her fist she clutched a withered dandelion. On the weed was a ball of fluff, just right for blowing.

When Tempe saw the dandelion a chill struck her, for she knew what Laurie was thinking. Tempe wished she had never told Laurie that rhyme about the dandelion. She walked briskly toward Laurie, planning to get her mind on something else. "Come on, let's get the socks for Granny."

Laurie didn't look up. She stared at the fluff. "Rhyme it for me, Tempe. I forget. Rhyme it."

Tempe picked up the basket. "Let's go."

"Say it!"

"It's a silly rhyme—"

"Tell me!"

Tempe sighed. Little girl with a long memory. Tempe recited in a hurry,

> *"Blow the weed*
> *And blow it well*
> *If Mother loves you*
> *Dandelion will tell."*

Then she said, "Let's go."

Laurie looked up. "I heard her calling. She said, 'Where are you?' "

Tempe frowned. "That was me calling you."

"She sang to me. The song had my name in it."

Tempe didn't know what to say, or what to do. Misery sharpened her voice. "For goodness sake, Laurie, that was *me* singing to you."

When Laurie began in a faraway voice, "Temp-ee . . ." Tempe knew what was coming. "When is Mother coming home?"

Tempe knelt. "I've told you, Laurie," she said in despair, "over and over—" Her voice broke. She did not hear approaching footsteps.

Laurie murmured, "I heard her calling me."

Another voice broke in—Father's. "Laurie, your mother can't come home again."

Tempe turned, flustered to see two anxious faces looking down at the girls, the faces of Father and Granny. She held up her empty hands. "I get so tired of telling her over and over." She let her hands drop. "Laurie won't believe me."

Granny took Laurie's hand and drew her to her feet. "I do declare," she said, trying to make her voice cheerful. "I get so lonesome in my house, not one chick a-chirping in it. How would you like to spend the night with me?"

Laurie turned quickly and put her hand in Tempe's. "I'll go if Tempe goes."

Granny said to Tempe, "Love to have you both, but we will ask your father."

Tempe looked at him. "Please. I'd like to go."

Father cleared his throat, and as was his custom, thought for a moment before speaking. Tempe was sure he would consent. "Sorry, girls," he said, "we need you both at home."

Tempe groaned and Laurie wailed. Granny's face showed her surprise.

Father held up his hand. "Don't howl. Come back to the house. I have something to tell the whole family."

Tempe felt excitement in the air. Three pairs of feet hurried to keep up with Father's long stride. Laurie ran on tiptoe. Granny's face was full of curiosity. "My goodness," she panted, "what's on your mind?"

CHAPTER 5

Tempe Herself

TEMPE AND LAURIE AND GRANNY GATHERED around Father on the porch. A gleam of fun was in his eyes, for he enjoyed their curiosity. Philip set down the iron. "What's up?" No one answered. Tempe kept her eyes on Father's face.

"Wasn't going to tell you until I was sure."

"Tell us?" Philip's voice rose and went off key. "Tell us what?"

"But I'm *pretty* sure now."

"My stars," murmured Granny.

"Phil and I worked on the thresher crew, just paying back the neighbors for help when our grain was harvested."

Grandpa nodded. "Trading work."

"That's right. The threshing machine belongs to the boss. Yesterday he told me he will take the machine to North Texas and Oklahoma. Grain is getting ripe there. He needs a few men to work for about six weeks, and he'll pay wages."

"Money?" Philip's voice slid up the scale. "Cash money?"

"Cash money." Father looked happy. "If we can earn wages for six weeks we can start building the lean-to rooms on this house."

"Well, glory be," said Grandpa.

"I spoke to him about you and me, Phil, for regular hands."

Philip's mouth dropped open. "Me? Money?"

Father grinned. "Wait—the boss said 'maybe.' He'll let us know for sure tomorrow."

Grandpa nodded his head. "Good workers, both of you."

"Phil's a good hand, a good helper. I told the boss, in a pinch, he could handle a wagon and team."

Granny sat in the rocker and beamed at Philip. "That's our boy! Spry as a June bug."

Tempe squirmed. Spry as a June bug, she thought, and twice as noisy. And mean—that was Philip.

She sat down. Father's eyes traveled from Philip to Tempe. "You are level-headed enough to hear some *maybe* news. If we don't get the job, don't be disappointed."

Tempe wondered why Father was looking so seriously at her; then she suddenly understood. If he and Phil went away, that would leave only Tempe and Laurie. Stay at home all alone every day for six weeks? Why, that was all summer! The thought made her mind spin.

Six long weeks without Father or Phil? But she didn't know how to milk Molly. And if she tried to use the big ax she'd chop her foot off. She and Laurie would be all alone in this empty house at night, listening to coyotes howl and worrying about prowling varmints. "My goodness," she began, but Father was still talking.

"I told the boss it was 'maybe' for us, too, until we talked it over."

Waiting for a pause Tempe almost choked. Abruptly she stood up and burst out, "My goodness sakes alive—"

Father could see what was on her mind. "Of course, we can't leave the girls here by themselves," he said. Tempe fell back into her chair.

It was Granny's turn to be upset. "Don't you know the girls are welcome at our house?" She pouted. "What's a granny for?"

"Thank you," Father said.

Granny was still sputtering. "My stars—"

Father held up his hand. "Now wait—there's more to think about. We can't go off and leave the cow and pig—"

"Talk, talk," muttered Granny.

Grandpa looked at Granny and said firmly, "*Somebody's* got to make plans."

Tempe couldn't listen to plans, for her mind went running ahead. All summer at Granny's house . . . why, she would be closer to Opal's, just a short walk. She couldn't wait! Exploring with Opal every day, eating at Granny's table, nothing to worry about. Granny would tell her when it was time to bring in wood and build a fire, and when to feed the chickens. Slowly she became aware of voices again. Grandpa and Father were deciding what to do.

". . . bring the stock to my place," Grandpa was saying.

Tempe whispered to Laurie, "Peter and Molly will go with us." Laurie clapped her hands noisily.

". . . I'll come over once a week and water your garden."

Granny grumbled, "Aren't you menfolks through with all that talkety-talk?"

Philip's eyes were feverish with excitement. Whistling shrilly through his front teeth, he danced a jig. He had to do *something* to *somebody*, so he grabbed Tempe by her shoulders. "Whee!" he shouted, and spun her like a top.

"You stop that!" Tempe slapped at him. "You leave me alone, now hear?"

Philip shouted, "I'm going to Oklahoma!" Turning to Father, he asked, "Will we see Indians in the Territory?"

"Maybe, I don't know."

Phil whooped like an Indian. He bent over and with hand to mouth, pranced through a war dance. Laurie came close and stared up at him. She did not smile.

"Cherokee, Choctaw, Chickasaw—" His voice began deep as a bass horn, but ended shrill as a fife. "Cherokee, Chocktaw, Chickasaw—" Phil stopped in front of Laurie, grinning all over his face, expecting to be admired.

"Did you like my Indian dance?"

Laurie stared solemnly at him and said nothing. Her mouth went down at the corners, but Phil didn't notice. In his eagerness, his voice climbed high again. "Did you like it?"

Laurie turned away from him. The family stopped talking. They waited to hear Laurie's answer. All was quiet on the porch. Phil leaned down closer to Laurie's face.

Laurie wrinkled her nose in disgust. Finally her voice came out in slow, measured words. "You—talk—like—a girl!"

Tempe laughed so hard she took the hiccups. Grandpa roared and slapped his knee. Granny joined in, and even Father was amused.

After the others quit laughing, Tempe couldn't stop. She rolled off the porch and fell in the dirt. Picking herself up and holding her ribs so they wouldn't ache, she went up the porch steps. Phil had collapsed in a chair, dropped his head and was silent. She marched up to him, pointed her finger at his nose and said in a voice that began low and ended high, "You—talk—like—a girl!"

Phil jumped from his chair, grabbed her arm, and pinned it behind her. She squawked like a chicken.

Father rose to his feet, grinned at Philip, and gave him a playful punch. "Leave your sister be. Girls don't like to rassle and fight."

He and Philip made fists and sparred, dancing about

45

on the porch with their brogans clumping noisily. They danced down the steps into the yard, like a couple of fighting roosters. Father's face looked as eager as Philip's. Laurie bubbled with laughter while Granny and Grandpa shouted encouragement.

"Get him, boy! Duck! Swing at him!"

Granny didn't enjoy staying on the sidelines. She couldn't rassle or box, but by Jingo she could sing!

"Rally in the canebrake
And shoot the buffalo!"

She put an arm in Laurie's and one in Tempe's.

"A play party!" Laurie squealed.

The three made a circle in the yard, singing and stamping their feet. After the boxing match ended, Philip and Father dropped on the steps, breathing hard. Granny tried to get them into the circle. Philip shook his head.

Father panted. "Can't—cut—the mustard."

Grandpa wouldn't budge at first, even when Granny nagged him, but when Laurie took his hand and pleaded, he could not refuse. She led him to the circle and they made a couple, tall Grandpa and tiny Laurie.

Tempe looked at Granny. "We're partners. Who plays the boy's part?"

"You're agile," said Granny, "you be the boy."

So Tempe, with her hair ribbons bouncing, swung Granny round and round. Hands clapped, feet pranced and voices chanted,

> *"Girls will cook and sew*
> *Boys will plow and hoe*
> *We'll rally in the canebrake*
> *And shoot the buffalo!"*

Tempe's ribbon bows fell off, and she finished the game with her hair loose and flying. Out of breath and panting, she dropped on the steps beside Father.

"Will you be glad to stay at Granny's?" he asked.

"Oh, yes." Her eyes shone. "I can't wait."

Father was silent for a moment. "I guess you'll be glad to get rid of Phil." As Tempe ducked her head, her hair fell forward. She was ashamed, but it was true.

Father sighed. "I hope after you've been apart for a while, you and Phil will appreciate each other."

"Um-hm," was all Tempe could say. She slipped off her shoes and wiggled her toes. She wanted to tell Father that it wasn't Phil she hated, just his bossy ways. Phil was her big brother. He was not afraid of anything in the dark, and sometimes he helped her with arithmetic.

Father said, "It's been sad for you and Laurie since"— his voice came from a tight throat—"since last winter." A bleak look came over his face. "It will help us all, I think, to be away."

Tempe, feeling her own throat tighten, could only nod.

After a moment, Father's natural voice came back.

"While we are gone, will you keep an eye on Laurie?"

"Oh, yes," said Tempe.

"A four-year-old changes fast. I hope Laurie will change." As he talked to her in a grownup way Tempe felt a thrill of pride. "If she asks about your mother coming home, you tell me when I get back."

"I will," said Tempe earnestly. "I sure will."

His face cleared. "It will be like a vacation for you at Granny's. You can be a child again."

Tempe stiffened. After all, she was almost eleven!

Father smiled. "Sorry." To make it up to her he put his big hand on her arm. That was almost like a hug, from Father.

Tempe kept her eyes down, staring at his hands. Hard work and sunburn had made them rough and brown, like harness leather.

"I mean at our house, you don't have enough time to play," he said. "At Granny's, for a while, you can be yourself."

Tempe could not look up. If she did, Father would see big tears forming under her eyelids. She nodded hard. A chance to be herself for the summer. Tempe herself, free, free, free!

CHAPTER 6

Time to Say Good-bye

TEMPE FELT LIKE HUGGING HERSELF. She had a room of her own—well, almost her own. Laurie was with her. It was Wednesday of the next week, and here they were, moved into Granny's spare bedroom.

Tempe, who had been up for an hour, looked around the room, counting their new luxuries. A soft rag carpet covered the floor. Laurie, who liked to lie on her stomach, was stretched out on the carpet now. White curtains fluttered at the window. The bed, with its spotless counterpane, was fat and comfortable. Here at Granny's, Tempe had hoped to sleep alone, but there was no extra bed. So she had settled into her old habit of sleeping with Laurie, who never stayed on her own side of the bed, and with Laurie's lumpy toys. Besides Butterflake, there was a new doll called Rags, a gift from Granny.

In the kitchen, Father and Philip were eating stacks of flapjacks and sorghum syrup. Tempe and Laurie had tried to eat breakfast, but the food would not go down.

Outside stood Father's wagon, packed with bedrolls, a camp stove, and clean clothes for him and Philip. The patient horses stood, hitched and ready to go. In the cool morning air they waited, quiet except for an occasional snort or a stamp of their big, iron-shod feet.

The other farm animals were not quiet this morning. Molly and her calf, the chickens, and Peter the pig had been moved to Grandpa's barnyard. They were alarmed by strange creatures in a strange place, especially by Grandpa's mule who sounded a loud "hee-haw" each morning and night. They were scared and homesick, and they talked about it. They talked plenty. From the barn came lonesome sounds—their bawls, squawks, and squeals.

In the house, too, were lonesome sounds. From the moment Laurie had seen the wagon and team waiting to take Father away, she had been tuning up to cry. Everybody knew what she would do when Father said goodbye. She would howl. It was Tempe's job this morning to "get Laurie's mind off it." She looked at Laurie sprawled on the floor, listless and whiny. It was impossible to make Laurie forget; she had a strong memory. Tempe drew a long breath.

"Laurie," she said, putting on a smile, "where's Butterflake?"

"Sick in bed."

"Want to play outside?"

"No."

"There's a big old mesquite tree in the back yard, easy to climb," Tempe told her. "Want to go see it?"

"No!"

"You won't fall. I'll hold you."

"No," said Laurie.

"Let's go see the chickens."

"No!"

But when Tempe held out her hand, Laurie clutched it, and on the way to the barn, squeezed hard. The hens were milling around in the pen. At every strange sound they fluttered and squawked.

Tempe told Laurie, "I'll have to give them a good talking-to," and she did. She leaned over the fence and began her lecture. "Listen here, ladies," she said in a sing-song voice, "stop worrying. You're in a new place, but Laurie and I, we're with you, same as always." The frightened clucks began to taper off. "You have plenty of food and water." Two hens scratched in the dirt. "Now just settle down and do some egg-laying."

Comforted, the hens began to hum a little. Some of them tilted their heads to look at Tempe with their odd, sideways glance. Tempe urged them, "I want you to lay lots of eggs. If you're too scared today, tomorrow will do." She turned to Laurie. "Why don't you talk to the lady hens?"

Laurie's mouth trembled. "Can we go in the wagon with Father?"

"Sorry, we have to stay here. Let's go talk to Molly and Peter."

Laurie was not interested in the cow or the pig. When

Tempe grabbed a big sunflower and stuck it behind Molly's horns to make Laurie giggle, Laurie hid her face in Tempe's skirt. Out of the corner of her eye Tempe saw Father and Philip at the gate, almost ready to leave. She tried all her tricks to cheer up Laurie. She twined three sunflower stalks into a wreath, put it around her own neck and danced along the path like a woodland sprite. Laurie did not laugh. Tempe handed the wreath to Laurie.

"They stink!" she wailed and threw them on the ground.

It was time to say good-bye. Father put an arm around Tempe. He didn't warn her to be a good girl. He smiled his slow smile and said, "We'll try to get back in time for your birthday." Tempe almost choked up. Her birthday. Father, too, had a strong memory.

He bent his knees and held out his arms to Laurie. She clung to his neck, begging to go. The wails and tears alarmed Philip and disgusted him. What's more, he wasn't giving *anybody* a good-bye hug. He crawled to the wagon seat, took the reins, and stared straight ahead. With a look of importance on his face he growled, "It's getting late." His voice began deep in his throat, but slid up scale to soprano. "Let's go!" Father joined Philip on the wagon seat. As Tempe led Laurie away, tears came to her own eyes.

"Good-bye, take care! Good-bye!" came the loud cries of the family as the wagon began to roll. Granny had a stack of old shoes to throw after the travelers, for good luck. Tempe threw shoes wildly and forgot her tears. Grandpa handed a shoe to Laurie. She refused to toss it, but her sobs dwindled.

As the family stood at the gate, waving at the disappearing wagon, the sun peeped over the treetops beyond the east pasture. On the morning air came the loudest cry of all. It came from the barnyard and was a long-drawn-out bray.

"Aw-w-eee-aww!" It was a wheeze, a snort, and a bellow, all combined. Grandpa's old mule, with his head over the gate, saluted the rising sun.

"Listen," Tempe told Laurie, "the old mule is telling Father and Philip good-bye!" Laurie stared at the mule, transfixed.

Grandpa asked, "Did you ever hear me go hee-haw?" Laurie turned to look at him. In spite of herself, she was interested. With hands at his temples Grandpa imitated the mule's long, restless ears. Bobbing his head up and down Grandpa gave out a harsh and noisy bray.

Laurie laughed!

Granny walked toward the house. When she thought nobody was looking she wiped her eyes on her apron. At the porch steps she turned. "Are you girls hungry? Let's go finish breakfast."

Tempe was surprised to feel a gnawing in her middle. "I'm starved." She ate flapjacks and two helpings of scrambled eggs.

CHAPTER 7

❦

Tempe's Collection

A POSTCARD FROM FATHER! Back from a walk to the rural mailbox, Grandpa put the card in Tempe's hand. Last week a letter had come telling the whole family the news of Father and Philip, but this card was addressed to Miss Tempe Foster. It was a personal message, and it read:

> Dear Tempe: Bad weather, muddy roads. Crops are late. The job will take longer than six weeks, so we will be home *after* your birthday. Your loving
> Father

It was a disappointment to Tempe, but not sharp enough to bring tears. Father couldn't keep his promise and was telling her ahead of time so she would understand.

Receiving mail pleased her—a message important enough to be written, stamped, and put in the post office. The card was something fine to show to the family and to Opal. On the other side of the card was a colored picture of a mustached gentleman wearing a dashing uniform, with boots, spurs, and a wide-brimmed hat. Why, it was a picture of President Roosevelt! The way he looked when he was leader of the Rough Riders, storming up San Juan Hill to victory. Just wait. When Opal saw this, her eyes would open wide.

In the weeks that followed each member of the Foster family received cards from Father. And there was a postcard from Philip. Not cards, just one card with a greeting to the whole family. It was smudged where Philip had erased and spelled over and erased again. The card read:

> Howdy Folks:
>   I earn cash money. Eats are good.
>   Yours respeckfully,
>   Mr. Philip Foster

Tempe sniffed. *Mister* Foster. "Huh," she grunted aloud, "I'll bet Father set him down and made him write it."

Grandpa reminded her, "But he *did* write it, didn't he?"

Living at Granny's was a delight, but it wasn't exactly the way Tempe had thought it would be. It was fun to be called in from play by the old plow bell. The bell was really an old iron plowshare, hung high from a rafter on the back porch. Grandpa had rigged it up years before, with a clapper made from a short piece of pipe.

It was like a church bell in a tower, Tempe thought. You pulled a long rope and made the bell ring. Ding, dong. When dinner was ready Granny rang the bell for everybody to come and eat. Father had told Tempe that when he was a boy, chopping cotton in the field, he listened all morning for the plow bell to call him home to dinner, and the morning seemed to go on forever.

Laurie wanted to ring the plow bell, and so did Tempe. Grandpa let the girls pull the rope twice apiece. After the four ding-dongs, he told them not to touch the bell rope. He said, "It's not a play-pretty. It's to call the family home quick, when you really need them."

Tempe understood Grandpa's rule about not touching the plow bell rope. She was used to rules, for she found rules at home with Father, at Opal's house, at school, and at church services. So, naturally, she expected Granny to have a list of rules and to tell her what they were. To Tempe's surprise Granny didn't say the rules out loud. She just let Tempe stumble along and bump into them. Bumping into Granny's rules kept Tempe puzzled much of the time.

Granny didn't say, "Keep the house tidy." No, that was not her way. Granny's way was to drop hints. When Tempe took off her sandals in the parlor and left them, she didn't find them later in the parlor. She found them in her room in the rocking chair.

Between meals Tempe liked to eat apples and peaches and cold chicken wings. One evening she found strange things on the seat of her rocking chair. Lying on an old newspaper were two apple cores, three peach seeds, and a heap of chicken bones. The chicken bones cured Tempe. She seldom forgot, after that, to put things where they belonged.

Granny's hints weren't all as plain as chicken bones. About other rules, Tempe had to guess. She was never sure just how Granny felt about her collected treasures. She and Opal caught a horned toad. Tempe put him on the back porch inside a box, gave him a pan of drinking water and spent an hour on her knees in the weeds, trying to catch bugs and flies to feed him. Granny sat on the porch with Laurie in her lap, rocking and cutting sideways glances at Tempe. When Tempe sat down, tired and warm, and with only two bugs for her trouble, Granny said to nobody in particular, "Catching bugs is hard on a human somebody."

"Why?" asked Laurie.

"It's not natural."

"Why not?"

"Now a horny toad, when he's free, can catch all the bugs and flies he wants, easy."

Tempe was tired and discouraged, and a little relieved to take Granny's hint. "All right," she said, "I wanted him for my collection, but I'll turn him loose."

She brought a snakeskin into the kitchen. It was a

flimsy, rustling thing in her hands, the snake's house after he had moved out. Granny rolled her eyes and shooed Tempe and the snakeskin out of the kitchen. "Hang it on the fence, belly side out. We need rain."

Tempe knew better than that. At the door she called back over her shoulder, "You hang a dead snake on the fence, not last year's skin."

Granny rattled pans on the stove. "We need rain," she said, bound to have the last word.

Tempe went outside, slow of step and kicking at pebbles. Did Granny really want her to have a collection? The next afternoon she found an old rusty horseshoe and showed it to Granny, who again sat in the porch rocker, with Laurie and her doll on the floor at her feet. Tempe asked if she could hang the rusty horseshoe in her room.

"Hang it over the gate," Granny said, "and keep the boogers away."

"What's boogers?" asked Laurie.

"Boogers are *bad*," said Granny, without explaining what boogers were.

"Boogers are *bad*," Laurie told Rags. Her eyes were shining, for she liked to talk about bad things and good things. She looked up at Granny. "Is a pooka good?"

"Some of the time."

"Is an elf good?"

"There's good elves and bad elves."

Laurie told Rags, "I have an elf. He lives in the mes-

60

quite tree but all day long he plays with me. His name is Greeny."

"You have three elves," Tempe told her, dropping down at the edge of the porch. By this time Grandpa had whittled with his sharp pocketknife and had made three elves, just like the story said. Tempe had stained the wood figures with green ink, oiled and polished them to a soft gleam.

"I have an elf," Laurie said. "His name is Greeny One, Greeny Two, Greeny Three. He plays with me, but he's *bad*. He made me spill the milk, he made me throw rocks at the chickens. He makes me so *mad!*" Laurie crawled into Granny's lap. She never tired of talking about the Little Folks. "Tell me, tell me," she begged.

Granny rocked. "Well, they're about this high." She measured vaguely with her hand. "And they're happy folks most of the time. They sing and eat and play wild games."

Laurie snuggled close to Granny. "Do they come around at night?"

"If you're good to them, they're good."

"Do they come around at night, and did you see them?" Laurie wanted to know.

Granny blinked her eyes and went on talking. "And if you hurt their feelings, they're full of mischief. They'll get even."

Laurie sat up straight, turned her head and gazed at Granny. "Did you ever see them?"

Granny never felt called upon to prove anything. If you doubted what she said, she ignored you. "Now if you go around turning over stumps looking for them, or calling, they won't answer, no sirree."

"Did you—" Laurie decided not to ask and dropped her eyes.

"And sometimes, when a whirlwind comes whirling along in the night, blowing shingles off the roof, well . . ."

Laurie was owly-eyed again, waiting for Granny to finish. Tempe waited, looking up from her seat at the edge of the porch, then asked, "Well?"

Granny rocked back and forth. The girls grew restless. "When folks stop and think about it—" She stopped rocking and looked wise. Her voice was slow and spooky. "They just *wonder who did it!*"

Tempe frowned. "You don't think the elves cause cyclones, do you?"

Granny looked down her nose at Tempe. "And who said anything about cyclones, Missy?" Tempe stared at the horseshoe in her hand, shaking her head. How on earth had the talk got around to cyclones? She had only asked if she could hang the horseshoe in her room.

From an exploring trip with Opal, Tempe had brought home a splendid black rock. Turning it from side to side, watching the light strike it from different angles, she was filled with wonder. It looked shiny blue-black one moment, murky-black the next. Grandpa said maybe it was volcanic rock. It was beautiful, Tempe thought, and a thing to be displayed on her dresser.

"Put it on the rock fence by the garden," said Granny. "It'll keep earthquakes away."

Tempe was hurt. How could Granny look upon her treasure as a common rock? Besides, who ever heard of earthquakes in Texas? The more she thought about it, the more injured she felt. Granny didn't like her treasures and wouldn't talk straight out to her.

She went in search of Grandpa and found him weeding the garden. "My collection!" she wailed. "It's scattered all over, or thrown away." She felt tears gathering. They embarrassed her, and to get rid of them she fumed. "If Granny doesn't want me to collect things, why doesn't she tell me plain? I'm not a little child! I can understand." Grandpa's eyes were sympathetic, so she went on, "And I never heard of such peculiar reasons she gives."

His eyes twinkled. "Your granny can always find a reason."

"But I don't know what to do with my collection!"

Grandpa laid down the hoe and put an arm around her shoulders. "Come with me," he said. With slow, sturdy steps he walked toward the windmill. "I know just the place."

CHAPTER 8

❧

A Compliment from Granny

HIGHER THAN THE HOUSE, HIGHER THAN the barn, the windmill tower pointed to the sky. At the top of the windmill was a giant wheel, and with it a long rudder. The wheel, the rudder, and the wind all worked together to turn the shaft and to pump water from the deep well.

Today the wheel was squeaking and spinning merrily, driven by a light wind. Sometimes, when the wind blew fierce and wild, whipping tree limbs about, the windmill clanked and groaned as it sent water rumbling through pipes and into the big round water tank. The water tank was off the ground about half as high as the mill wheel. Some people built high platforms, like stilts, for their water tanks to sit on. Years before, Grandpa had built a little room with rock walls, and on top of the room had placed his water tank.

Grandpa led Tempe to the rock room, opened the door and invited her to look inside. Bridles, harness, and a saddle hung on the walls. There was nothing in the middle of the room. "Now," he asked, "if there was a table in here, would it hold your collection?"

Tempe brightened. "Oh, Grandpa, it's perfect! Do you have a table?"

"I can set two nail kegs on the floor, lay an old door across—"

Tempe was overjoyed. "When? Where?"

"Any time you want them, bring them from the barn."

"A playhouse! Just what I've always wanted. Just wait until I show Opal!"

The next day when Opal peered into the little rock room she balanced on her toes for a moment, breathless, then squealed, "Oh, Temp!" As she whirled to face Tempe her mane of bright hair spun around. "Is it really ours?"

With Opal's help Tempe rounded up all her treasures —the arrowheads, the rocks, the snakeskin, and the bird's nest. They gathered up their paper dolls and placed them in family groups on the table. Laurie brought her dolls and the three elves.

They began to play in earnest. Opal's hair fell forward as they cut out more paper figures. Tempe's brow wrinkled while she pinned paper dresses on paper dolls. But a rude wind whistled in through the open door and disturbed the paper dolls. Tempe closed the door only to find she had shut out the breeze and most of the light. Laurie soon left them to sit in a fork of the old mesquite tree and sing lullabies to her dolls. In the stifling heat Tempe and Opal stared at each other. Their faces were glum, their voices doleful.

"We can't see—dark."

"Yes."

"Hot—"

"Yes, too hot."

Perspiration gathered on the girls' faces, their arms, and on their legs. Tempe said, "We could move everything outside in the shade of the tree."

So they labored the rest of the afternoon. They cleared the table, rolled the nail kegs out into the blessed moving air, laid the door across and transferred the rocks, the horseshoe, the snakeskin, the arrowheads, and the bird's nest. The last thing they moved was the group of paper dolls.

Opal bounced back to her old cheerful self. "This is perfect!" she gloated, as a lively breeze cooled her brow.

Tempe was not so sure. "It's better, I guess," she said, laying out the Mrs. Jones family of dolls and the Mrs. Smith family, anchoring them with small rocks.

But the same south wind that refreshed the girls and dried their perspiring faces swooped down toward the paper dolls. It picked up the Jones children and the Smith children, tossing them high in the air. The girls scrambled to capture the paper dolls, but the frisky wind cheated them. Every scrap of paper sailed over their heads, past the fence, beyond the garden, and disappeared. Just like that. One moment Tempe's hands were filled with paper children, the next her hands were empty.

"I give up!" she wailed, ready to cry.

Opal refused to mope. "Playing dolls is tacky anyhow," she said. "Let's climb."

So they climbed all over the old mesquite tree. Laurie, afraid to climb, was content to sit in the tree fork, gnaw a green tomato from the garden, and talk to her elves. "We eat in a tree, sleep in a tree, live in a tree—"

Tempe and Opal explored the gnarled limbs and cozy forks of the sprawling mesquite. There was a wing to the right and a wing to the left; there were places to sit and play and limbs to swing from.

Grandpa strolled by. "Watch out for thorns on mesquite limbs," he told the girls. They looked at each other and giggled, then showed him a scratch on Opal's leg and a tear in Tempe's dress. He brought out his pocket-knife. "We'll dethorn the limbs where you climb," he said. The girls searched for thorns and Grandpa did most of the cutting. At Tempe's pleas to help cut off the thorns he dug deeper in his pockets and found his second-best knife with a duller blade. "All right," he said, handing it up to her. "Use this, and be careful."

After the job was finished and Grandpa had gone to the house, Opal said, "I never saw such a big mesquite tree."

"It's old and it spreads out like a house."

"Sure," said Opal, "a house of many rooms."

A sudden idea struck Tempe. "A tree house!" she shouted. "Let's build a tree house."

"When? How?"

"Right now."

But a sound came from the house, clang, clang. Granny's plow bell. Tempe frowned. "What? It's too early for supper."

They climbed down, and from the back porch Granny announced, "It's four-thirty, Opal, and your mama said always to tell you when to go home."

Opal dawdled, of course, but around five o'clock, while the fiery sun still beat down from the western sky, she waved to Tempe from the north lane.

"Don't forget!" she said. "Tomorrow, we build the tree house."

That evening after supper Tempe sat on the steps, thought about her specimens, and was happier than she had been for a long time. Her poor homeless treasures were all in one spot now, under the mesquite tree, and soon would have a settled place of their own. Displayed in the tree house they would make a handsome collection. She was pretty sure now how Granny felt about her specimens; she didn't want them in the house. But why hadn't Granny told her, straight out?

The screen door opened, and Granny's long skirts rustled toward the porch chair. "You're happy tonight, aren't you?" she asked.

"Yes'm," said Tempe, thinking Granny was always alive to her moods.

"I'm glad you found a place for your play-pretties."

"Granny, why didn't you *tell* me you didn't want them

in the house?"

The creaking rocker became still. In gathering darkness Tempe could not read Granny's face; she had only her words, and they were slow in coming. "When a body's almost eleven," Granny said soberly, "she isn't a child anymore." Now what did she mean by that? There was another long pause. "Eleven years old is a good age," said Granny in a lighter tone, "young enough to like horny toads and old enough to understand without a lot of talkety-talk."

Tempe was silent for a while, pondering. She had overheard Granny, in talking with grownups, use hints to spare their feelings. Old enough to understand . . . why, Granny had paid her a compliment!

She took a long breath and let it out slowly, as her thoughts unwound. Horned toads didn't fascinate Granny the way they fascinated Tempe. Granny didn't want rocks and bones and snakeskins and goodness knows what else in her tidy house. So she had dropped hints, in the roundabout way she used with grownups, to spare Tempe's feelings.

Tempe jumped up and put her arms around Granny. "I'll bet you think I'm pretty slow, not to catch your hints."

The dusk deepened. Tempe sat down again, leaned against a porch column and curled into a knot with her knees under her chin. The familiar night sounds—the chirp of crickets and the swish of tree limbs restless in

69

the breeze—all faded out. Tempe felt alone and suspended in the quietness, a quietness so deep she could
feel, with her hands under her throat, the beating of her
own pulse.

The rocking chair was still, and out of the blackness
came Granny's misty voice. The words had no beginning
and no end, they just hung there. Tempe held her breath.
"Lots of times, a body doesn't need to speak . . . the
one listening doesn't need to hear . . . if she listens with
her heart."

CHAPTER 9

✠

The Right Name

TOMORROW CAME, THE DAY TO BUILD the tree house, but there was no Opal. Tempe climbed the mesquite tree and looked toward Opal's house. There was no blue calico sunbonnet bobbing along in the pasture.

"Maybe Opal's sick," Tempe worried, "or mad at me."

Granny was calm. "No cause to think that. Folks get busy. She'll be back."

Tempe did not want to begin the tree house alone, so she spent her time looking around Grandpa's barn for more treasures. She found a joint of rusty pipe and hung it over a limb of the tree. Struck with a rock it made a ringing sound, almost like Grandpa's plow bell. It was a fine, loud sound. She couldn't wait for Opal to hear it.

On the third morning, when the sun was a quarter high, Tempe gave up looking for Opal's sunbonnet. But just as she settled down in the kitchen to help Granny shell black-eyed peas, Opal appeared at the back gate, warm and thirsty. Tempe bounced up, spilling peas, and led her inside.

"We've had company," Opal explained, "cousins from

East Texas."

Granny nodded. "Told you so."

Tempe gave Opal a drink of cool water. "Hurry," she said, "got something to show you."

"Let the child get her breath," said Granny.

While Opal drank, Tempe thrashed around the floor on hands and knees picking up the peas. She threw them in the pan and fidgeted while Opal thanked Granny in a polite tone for the drink. Then she grabbed Opal's hand and led her out the back door and to the mesquite tree.

They climbed high. When Opal heard the pipe bell ring, she was delighted. She clanged, and Tempe clanged. Tempe stood high on a mesquite limb and sang,

"My country 'tis of thee
Sweet land of liberty—"

Opal rang the pipe bell, clang, clang.

Tempe struck a pose. As she sang, her left hand lay on her chest and her right hand pointed to the sky.

"—from every mountain side
Let freedom ring."

Clang, clang, clang, went their bell.

Tempe was in a heroic mood—a wild, free mood. "If we had a flagpole, I'd raise a flag."

"Sure," said Opal, "if we had a flag."

"Let's make speeches."

Opal, the best memorizer at school, recited *Paul Revere's Ride*. Tempe remembered the brave words of Colonel Travis at the Alamo. Climbing as high as she dared in the tree she shouted, "I shall never surrender or retreat!"

"Victory or death!" quoted Opal.

This led to a game of "Alamo." Tempe was Colonel Travis, and Opal was Davy Crockett. They defended the fort amid groans of dying men; they shot the cruel enemy. Their shouts excited Laurie. Won over by the struggle of "good men against bad men" she begged to join the game. Tempe told her she could play the part of Mrs. Dickenson.

"Run, Laurie!" Tempe called out. "You and your baby—escape the Alamo!" Clutching Rags in her arms, Laurie ran to safety while Tempe and Opal died bravely in a pool of their own blood.

By this time they were certain they could build a fort or a castle, but decided to follow their plan and build a tree house. They cleared off the old door that Grandpa had given them. How could they lift it into the tree? The main trunk of the mesquite forked at a spot no higher than their heads, making two trunks, one leaning to the left and the other to the right. They decided to take the door up the slope on the left side of the tree. With Tempe holding one end of the door and Opal the other, they tried to haul it up. The door was too heavy.

Laurie stood around, looking lost. Tempe told her, "Out of the way—scoot!" Laurie's mouth trembled. Tempe found a rope, tied it to the door knob, threw the rope over a limb. Both girls pulled, grunting and perspiring.

"A little higher, Temp!" groaned Opal.

The door was dangling in the air, almost high enough to make a tree perch, when they heard a splintering sound. Screws gave way, and the rusty door knob fell out, taking the whole lock. The door crashed to the ground. Laurie howled with fright and ran to the house. Tempe and Opal sat down hard on the ground with the rope limp in their hands. Tempe almost cried, but when Opal giggled she decided to laugh. They laughed until they collapsed on the ground.

Opal sat up first and pushed hair out of her eyes. "Ugh!" she said in disgust, noticing her grimy hands, "I'm a mess," and with a quick look at Tempe, "and so are you!"

Staring at each other, they saw dirt-streaked faces, rumpled dresses, and tousled hair, a sight which sent them into more shrieks of laughter.

"Oh, who cares?" Tempe had her breath back now and was staring at the door. "Look, a hole in the door! A hole where the lock fell out. We'll put the rope through the hole and pull the door up again."

Opal rubbed a bruised elbow. "Aw, Temp—again?"

Tempe got to her feet and struck her heroic pose. "We

shall never surrender or retreat!"

"Aw, Temp—"

After a rest, they began again. Pull, push, groan, grunt, and this time the door dangled high over their heads. Tempe asked, "Can you hold it there? I'll climb up and swing the door around to make a shelf."

Opal braced her feet in the dirt and hung on to the rope. Setting her jaw she grunted, "I've got it!"

Tempe bounced into the tree and struggled with the dangling door. Carefully she maneuvered it until it rested flat and level across two strong limbs. "Hey, look!" she called out, "it's perfect." She gingerly stepped on the door. No jiggle, it was steady. She sat on it and swung her feet in the air. "Come up and try it!" Trailing green mesquite branches sheltered the spot from the sun. "It's our tree house!"

Cautiously Opal sat on the board. "It will hold, I guess."

"We'll put a heavy rock at each corner."

And they did. Anchored by rocks, the board was quite steady. Perspiring, the girls hauled up their treasures— the pincushion cactus, the volcanic rock, the arrowheads, the rusty horseshoe, the snakeskin, and the bird's nest. There was barely room to sit down.

Laurie came back and tried to join them on their perch. The climb frightened her, and she backed down, complaining, "Want to see. Me and Rags, want to see."

Tempe saw Granny on the porch and called, "Come

look! See what we built."

"My land," said Granny in amazement, staring upward, "what have you got there?" She circled the tree. "What's holding it up?"

"Tree branches," said Tempe proudly.

"What's holding it down?"

"Rocks," Opal told her. "Heavy rocks."

"My stars!" As Granny took in this unbelievable sight she backed away a few feet, grabbed Laurie and held her close to her own skirts.

Laurie pointed. "Want to see up there—"

"Come down, Tempe," Granny said firmly, "this minute."

Tempe was astonished. Granny must be joking. She stared at Opal, who stared down at Granny's serious face.

"Come down, Opal."

"Yes, ma'am," said Opal soberly, and got to her feet.

Tempe tried to explain. "Grandpa don't care. He gave us the door."

"Down, Tempe." She pointed to the barn. "Go fetch your grandpa."

Tempe ran to the barn, shaking her head all the way. Grandpa would understand, she thought. "We did it!" she told him proudly. "We just wore ourselves out—"

Looking at Tempe's wild hair he said, "I can see that."

"But we did it!"

Back at the tree they found Granny serious of face, Opal glum, and Laurie in tears. Grandpa listened to

Tempe's story and followed her pointing finger. He scratched his head and circled the tree, looking up. Tempe ran out of words and waited for him to speak. They all waited.

Grandpa straightened his glasses on his nose and said, "Pretty good job there, girls!" They sighed with relief. Why had Granny made such a fuss? "Have to brag on you girls. Hard work, hauling that door into the tree." They grinned. Tempe stole a look at Granny and smirked. But Grandpa went on, "I'll brag on your granny too. She knows something I know. Your playhouse isn't safe!"

Granny's face now wore a smug smile. Tempe's hope fell hard, with a thud. "Safe?" she asked faintly.

"Nothing's holding it."

"Oh—oh," breathed Tempe and Opal together, like air leaving a balloon.

"Just heavy rocks. One wrong move, and your whole playhouse will tumble."

Grandpa brought a ladder, his box of tools and wire. He lashed the door securely to the tree branches. Soon the platform was steady and strong, anchored with three guy wires. Looking at the dangling joint of pipe he said, "I'd better tie that to the limb." After the pipe was secure he struck it with his hammer. "Let freedom ring," he quoted, winking solemnly at the girls.

When Tempe and Opal went in the house to get a cool drink Granny said, eyeing their smudged faces and unruly hair, "You girls look like a cyclone hit you," which

persuaded them to clean up and comb their hair. Back at the tree they climbed like monkeys while Laurie, earthbound and forlorn, gazed up at them.

She complained, with one plump arm raised, "I want up." The girls didn't listen; Grandpa didn't listen. She opened her mouth wide, threw back her head and shouted, "Me and Rags—up!" Not one head turned. Laurie's knees stiffened; she shut her eyes tight, swung her hair violently from side to side and bawled, "Help me up, up, up—UP!"

Grandpa put his hands over his ears. "All right, I heard you." As her bawling let up he looked over the top of his glasses. "How would you like to saddle up the old gray mare?"

Laurie calmed down. Grandpa brought an old saddle from the barn. It was battered and stiff like an old shoe left out in the weather, and had long since lost its stirrups. Grandpa threw it over a low-hanging limb and made it secure with a strong rope. Laurie climbed into the saddle. "A mile and a half," she announced. "I'll ride a mile and a half. Rags wants to go, and Butterflake, and the elves—"

Grandpa called out to Tempe, "Go to the corncrib and bring back that splint basket." Tempe obeyed. Into the basket went Laurie's dolls and the three elves. The basket hung within easy reach of Laurie's hand. Grandpa asked, "Everybody satisfied now?"

Nobody heard his question; nobody answered. They

were all too busy. Laurie rode the old gray mare, then Grandpa's mule, then the pooka, singing, "A mile and a half, a cow and a calf."

Tempe, back in the tree with Opal, sat cross-legged on their shady perch, sorting arrowheads. When she saw Grandpa tramping away she jumped to her feet. "My goodness, I didn't say 'thank you.'" She ran down and hugged his neck.

The sun slid down fast, and Opal had to go home. After Tempe gathered eggs and fed the chickens, the cows and the pig, she sat for a while in the tree house, feeling happy. A few feet below, in her saddle seat, Laurie chattered.

Living at Granny's had proved to be the way Father said, Tempe thought; it was being herself, happy and free. She did all her chores here, but the chores didn't worry her. If she forgot, Granny and Grandpa reminded her. If she didn't know how to do a task, they were always there, ready to explain.

The tree was a fine place. She could see the whole world from here. It was a high, brave place, and it deserved a brave name. She would talk it over with Opal. The songs they had sung and the game they had played went around and around in her mind, like a turning wagon wheel. Sweet land of liberty, of thee I sing, clang, clang. Let freedom ring, clang, clang . . . Tempe reached above her head and gently tapped the pipe bell. Maybe the name should be Liberty Tree, or Freedom

Tree. They would vote on it. If it became a tie vote they would let Laurie decide. Laurie didn't know what liberty or freedom meant, but she could vote.

Tempe listened to Laurie's chatter drifting up from below. Dusk had fallen. Birds, with heads under their wings, were hushed. Fireflies twinkled in the blackness. From the limb below came a small voice.

"Let's go to sleep, now," Laurie crooned. "Hush now. I'm holding you in my lap, and the Mother Tree is holding me in *her* lap. Hush now—"

Tempe sat very still. There would be no vote. The tree that sheltered them had a name, and it was the right name. Laurie didn't know much, but she could feel, and feeling was sometimes stronger than knowing. Laurie couldn't feel anything about liberty or freedom, but she had a feeling for the sprawling old mesquite tree which had put its sheltering arms around her. She called it the Mother Tree.

CHAPTER 10

Do As You Wish

TEMPE TOLD OPAL THAT LAURIE HAD NAMED the old mesquite the Mother Tree.

"That's a good name," said Opal, not wondering for a moment why Laurie chose the name. But Tempe wondered.

Tempe wondered if the ache in Laurie's heart for Mother had made her feel the name. Laurie seemed content at Granny's. A chatterbox, she talked and talked—to the family, to the elves, and to her dolls. Not once had Laurie asked, "When will Mother come home again?" She often tried to get Tempe to join her games of pretend. "Will you play like with me?" she asked. "Will you be the mother?"

Tempe had her own games. "Ask Granny to play like a mother."

Laurie laughed. "Silly!" She pointed a finger at Tempe. "You're silly."

"What's silly about it? Granny likes to pretend."

Laurie's nose wrinkled. "She can't be a mother. She's a granny."

As the summer days hurried along, Tempe, too, was cheerful at Granny's. The memory of Mother did not bring a heavy ache to her heart. Looking at an empty rocking chair in Granny's parlor did not hurt. Listening to the wind that wailed down Granny's stovepipe did not remind her of Mother's calling voice. She told Opal, one cheery morning in Granny's back yard, "Father was right. It helps to be away from our old house for a while."

"I'm glad," said Opal.

"But I'm not sure about Laurie. I wish I knew why she named the mesquite the Mother Tree."

"Why don't you ask her?"

Tempe shook her head. "Then she might ask when Mother will be home."

"Ask her in a roundabout way."

Tempe brightened. "A good idea." She looked across the yard at Laurie, who played at the base of the mesquite surrounded by her toys. "Let's go."

Tempe tapped with her knuckles on the tree trunk. "Knock, knock," she said, "may I come in?"

Laurie asked hopefully, "Are you going to play with me?"

Tempe nodded toward Laurie's toys. "Do you and your children live in this house?"

Laurie did not answer.

"What is the name of your house?"

Laurie stared at Tempe and said nothing.

It was Opal's turn to tap on the tree. "Knock, knock,"

she said in a bright voice, "we're looking for Mrs. Laurie and her children."

Laurie slowly turned toward Opal, but did not answer. Her mouth drooped almost to a pout.

Opal tried to win her over with a smile. "Mrs. Laurie, may we play with your children in the Mother Tree?"

Laurie's answer was a blank stare. She turned to Tempe. "Will you play like with me?"

"Play like? That's what we're trying to do."

Laurie grasped Tempe's hand. "Will you play like the mother? Me and Butterflake and Rags and Sissy—we'll mind you."

Tempe looked down into Laurie's pleading face, then across at Opal. She shrugged. "Well, maybe, for a little while."

Instantly, Laurie became the cheerful chatterbox again. "You can tell us what to do. Sit over here, we'll make room." Laurie swept her dolls from an apple crate. Her voice became high and loud, a tone she used for pretending. "Butterflake, move over, let Mother sit down. Rags, you and Sissy be quiet, or Mother will scold."

Tempe sat on the box. "I never heard you talk about Sissy before. Who is she?"

"Sissy is my sister. She's—"

Tempe rolled her eyes. "Your sister?"

"Sissy is my sister and we sleep together, eat together—"

"But *I'm* your sister," said Tempe.

"Sissy is my sister, she's four years old, and—" As Opal dropped to the ground beside the dolls, Laurie frowned. "You're sitting on Sissy."

"Excuse me." Opal stole a look at Tempe, trying not to smile.

The older girls were a little bored with Laurie's game, but since they had started the idea, they played it in grand style. Tempe gave orders to everyone. Opal pretended to disobey, got a spanking and had to sit in the corner with Sissy, Laurie's imaginary sister. Laurie was enchanted by the game and would have played it all day.

After half an hour Tempe and Opal begged off. As they strolled toward the house Tempe sighed. "We didn't learn a thing. I still don't know why Laurie named the old mesquite the Mother Tree."

The more Tempe thought about the name, the better she liked it. The Mother Tree was strong and good. It sheltered them like a home. In the tree nobody complained, "You're too noisy," or "You're crowding me." There was room on the low limbs for Laurie and room on the high limbs for the older girls.

One morning Opal brought a message from her mother. "She says for you to visit at my house."

Tempe asked, "Are you tired of the tree house?"

"No, but Mama says tree house or not, it's my turn to have company."

Granny agreed that turnabout was fair and right. Opal whispered, "Ask your granny if you can stay all night with

85

me." Granny agreed to that plan, too. Tempe whooped with joy, hugged Granny, and ran to tell Grandpa. He beamed, Opal glowed, and everything seemed settled.

But nobody had asked Laurie what her feelings were. They soon found out. Laurie sat on the back steps with a doll under each arm, listened quietly to the plans, then began to howl. Tempe put her arms around her. "I'm not going now. I'll go late this afternoon and be back with you tomorrow." Laurie's wails did not stop. At Opal's distress Tempe said, "Never mind. She will forget all about it by the time we leave."

They thought of something to get Laurie's mind off it. Holding Laurie's hands in theirs, they carefully led her up the trunk of the Mother Tree. At the top she crowed with delight, sat on the old door and swung her feet over the edge. With a sunny smile she waved to Granny, who watched from the porch.

Tempe whispered, "See, she's all right now."

But when shadows grew long, when the girls whispered of leaving, Laurie disappeared into the house. Opal waited on the back steps while Tempe went to her bedroom to change her clothes. Tempe heard sobbing. It was not howling, but a steady, quiet crying. She looked in the closet, behind the door, then under the bed. On the rag carpet, rolled into a knot and clutching two dolls, was Laurie. To Tempe's pleading, she would not come out, so Tempe crawled under the bed. Questioned, Laurie said she could not sleep alone.

"But you'll have your dolls. And with me gone, you'll have room for the elves."

The elves were too bad to sleep with, Laurie told her. "We're afraid," she wailed.

"Who's we?"

"Me and Butterflake and Rags and Sissy."

Nothing Tempe said changed Laurie's mood. Tempe lost patience. "Oh, Laurie, don't be a crybaby!" But the crying did not stop.

Tempe crawled out and with a sinking heart went to look for Granny and Grandpa. They would make her stay at home, she fumed to herself, and it wasn't fair. She found them in the vegetable garden and told them that Laurie had spoiled everything. Following them back to the house, she was sure she knew what their answer would be.

To her surprise, Granny and Grandpa went into the kitchen and whispered together. Tempe waited in the parlor, fidgeting. Grandpa came out and looked down at her over his glasses. His face was very serious. He cleared his throat and gave her news that surprised her even more. "It would not be fair to tell you what to do, Tempe," he said. "You are free to decide. Do as you wish, and we will agree."

Tempe gulped and sputtered, trying to understand. It was hard to believe that they were not going to give her any orders. Weak-kneed, she dropped into a chair. She didn't know what to do. She rose, followed Grandpa into the kitchen and stood around, first on one foot and then the other. Grandpa sat at the table with a newspaper in his hands. Granny, with her back toward Tempe, began to peel potatoes. They said nothing. Tempe wished they would tell her what to do, but they did not.

Suddenly, Tempe was angry. She was angry at Laurie for being a crybaby and spoiling her plans. She was angry because nobody would decide for her what to do. She forgot her manners. While Opal waited patiently on the back steps, Tempe ducked her head to hide angry tears and ran for the Mother Tree. She climbed to the tree house and stared toward the setting sun. It wasn't fair, it wasn't fair!

After ten minutes had passed Granny came out, reminded her of her duty and returned to the house. Tempe sniffed hard, straightened her shoulders and crawled down. She had nothing planned to say to Opal, who by now was waiting at the gate, sunbonnet in hand. Tempe walked like a wooden doll, not knowing what was in her own mind. But at the gate, Opal's smile waited for her. Opal's hand reached out toward Tempe.

She took the outstretched hand, returned Opal's smile, and found herself saying, "Sorry, but I have to stay with Laurie. She depends on me."

CHAPTER 11

❦

Free As an Angel

BY THE NEXT WEEK TEMPE HAD MADE another plan. Both she and Laurie would go to Opal's house and spend the day. The new plan suited everybody.

At Mrs. Ford's house Laurie played with Opal's little brothers who were three and five years old. That left the older girls free during the long day.

Opal led Tempe into her room and showed her a treasure. While washing the dishes one day, Opal said, her mother had broken a beautiful cut glass pitcher. Mrs. Ford almost cried, for it had belonged to her grandmother. A family heirloom, it was now in half a dozen pieces. Opal begged for the broken pitcher. Only one piece of the heavy cut glass was safe to play with, her mother said. She gave Opal the largest piece of glass. On the fragment was the curving pitcher handle.

"Listen to this," Opal told Tempe. She held the fragment lightly in her left hand and tapped it with her right index finger. The glass gave out a lilting song. Tempe was delighted. The girls ran a string through the handle and tied the piece of cut glass over the doorway to Opal's room. They made countless trips in and out of the room, tapping the glass with a fingernail and listening to its musical chime.

Tempe loved the chime, for it was delicate and haunting, like fairy music. She pictured it in the tree house, suspended from an overhead branch, swaying in the breeze, adding a touch of magic to her retreat. She longed for the chime, but she tried not to act envious, or to *look* envious.

That evening when she and Laurie were ready to go home Opal took down the cut glass chime and put it in Tempe's hand. Tempe was overcome with shame. "No, no!" She returned the chime and backed off. "Did it show?" she asked anxiously. "In my face, I mean?"

Opal pretended she didn't know what Tempe meant. "I'll loan it to you for the summer, to hang in the Mother Tree."

A loan, and only for the summer; Tempe was relieved. This way, she could accept the chime. Tenderly she carried it home. She tried it out in six different places before she found exactly the right spot, a place her hand could reach while she was sitting or lying down in the tree house.

Tempe and Laurie visited Opal's home many times. The older girls skipped rope, played in the hay loft or sat on bales of hay and talked while Opal hemmed napkins. Every day Opal had to sew a little, part of her training in how to keep house.

Sewing! Tempe looked uneasily at Opal, who was making dainty stitches, talking and smiling all at the same time. Tempe thought her own fingers would never learn the knack, but one day she tried it. Her stitches were not as straight as Opal's, but she found that sewing was not as bad as she had feared.

Perched on a stack of baled hay, Tempe dangled her legs and confided, "Now that I'm used to the place, I love it at Granny's. I can be myself."

Opal sat up straight like a lady, her fingers moving in a delicate way, as she made tiny stitches. "Can't you be yourself at home?"

"No!" Tempe's harsh voice brought a shocked look to Opal's face. Tempe hurried to explain, "It's Philip—he tries to boss me."

Explaining did not erase Opal's doubt. "Can't you be yourself at home while the men work in the field?"

As Tempe frowned and searched for words, her restless heels bumped the bale of hay. "At home, just me and Laurie, I *worry*."

"Worry about what?"

"I'm afraid I'll forget things. Nobody's there to remind me. At Granny's they tell me when to bring in wood and gather the eggs."

Opal didn't quite understand, Tempe reflected later as she and Laurie walked home. That was natural, for Opal didn't have Tempe's kind of worries, and she didn't have a big brother.

On Monday morning a letter from Father arrived, saying that he and Philip would be home in about four weeks. Tempe's heart leaped for a moment with the thought of having Father back again, then her joy faded. She would have only four more weeks to be truly herself.

She thought of the old house, of Phil's cruel teasing, and of the lonely days at home, with only Laurie beside her. She felt hemmed in. She wanted to be somebody else, not the girl who must go back to Father's kitchen and struggle with heavy iron pots on the wood range.

The hemmed-in feeling would not leave, even when Opal arrived later in the day. It grew into a sort of panic, making Tempe loud and boisterous. From the highest limb of the mesquite tree she chanted, "Four more weeks, four more weeks!" Swinging her feet in rhythm, she shouted, "I need four more months!"

Opal took up the chant. "Four more weeks, four more months—"

Tempe jumped to her feet. "Four more months, four more years, I'll be free!"

Laurie wanted to share their excitement. She left her saddle seat and fearfully climbed the limb toward the other girls. Gasping with fright she echoed, "Free, free—" Her chant became a wail. "Tempe, help me up!"

Tempe climbed nimbly down to meet Laurie, took her hand and hoisted her to the tree house perch. The three girls sat in a row with their feet dangling. Laurie broke into smiles. Tempe struck the pose of an orator and

shouted, "Four more weeks of liberty!"

"Liber-tee!" Laurie echoed.

"Free as an eagle!" said Tempe, with her right hand pointing toward the sky. Opal's reply was slow in coming. She frowned, struggling with an idea. Tempe pounded her own chest and repeated, "Free as an eagle!"

Opal's face cleared. "Free as an angel!"

"Angel!" echoed Laurie.

Tempe seized upon Opal's idea. "Free as an angel with a golden harp!" She leaped to her feet and twanged on an imaginary harp. "Free as an angel. I'll never go home again. I'll never boil the beans and cook the corn bread. I'll never go back! I'll stay right here forever and play my harp." Caught up in her own fancy, she paid little mind to the others. She shouted until out of breath, then turned to see a sober look on Opal's face. She panted, "What's the matter—with you?"

Opal asked anxiously, "You won't go home to your father?"

Until now Tempe had not really believed what she was saying. But Opal's shocked look goaded her pride. Tossing her head she said, "I certainly will not!"

"Oh, Tempe!"

Opal's gentle scolding stung Tempe, but she would not give in. "I'm staying in the Mother Tree!"

It was plain that Opal had a different opinion, for she dropped her part in the boisterous play, rose and got ready to climb down.

Tempe scowled, thinking what a goody-goody face Opal had. Aloud she said, "Are you telling me I am wrong?"

Opal would not answer. When pressed, she nodded her head briefly.

The sting of Opal's nod made Tempe explode. "The nerve of you!" She knew she was insulting her best friend but she couldn't stop. "Goody-goody Opal!" she heard her gabbling mouth say. "Can't tell me what to do. I'm staying in the Mother Tree forever and ever!"

Laurie's voice echoed, "Forever and ever."

Opal told Tempe sadly, "You shouldn't say bad things in front of Laurie."

Tempe stuck out her chin. "And what did I say that is bad?"

Opal said slowly, "Like being sassy and not minding what your folks tell you to do."

"You're pretty sassy yourself, Miss Goody-face!"

Opal looked shocked at first, then her face turned pink. After a long pause she came back with, "Well—I'm not a stubborn mule like you!"

Tempe leaped on that. "A stubborn mule? Then you're as dirty as a dog full of fleas!"

Opal was thinking fast now. "You're as smelly as a skunk!"

"You're as nasty as a goat!"

"—sneaky as a snake!"

"—greedy as a filthy hog!"

"You wallow in the mud!"

"You honk and gabble like a goose!"

"You strut like a turkey gobbler!"

Laurie showed whose side she was on. Twining her arms around Tempe she glared at Opal. "You can go home now!"

Tempe had run out of breath and had run out of insults, and now she was filled with terror. Opal would go home and never, never, come back. Opal would run away and leave her. Opal wasn't a friend anymore. All right, Tempe told herself, if Opal felt that way, she was glad to be rid of her.

"I'm sorry I ever met you!" she told Opal hotly. "I'm sorry I wasted my time on you. You're no friend. Laurie is right, go on home where you belong!"

Close to tears, Opal climbed down from the tree, ran to the back gate and headed for home.

Tempe could not move. Her wild words, the words she could not bring back, made a prisoner of her. She turned her face in the other direction and let her best friend go away without a word of good-bye.

Laurie grew restless and begged to be helped out of the tree. Tempe did not move. Laurie gathered courage to crawl backward down the slope, squealing with fear, pleading for help. Tempe ignored her. On the ground again, Laurie called out, "I'm down!" No answer came. "Temp-ee!" With a lonesome wail Laurie ran toward the house and Granny.

Laurie would tell on her, thought Tempe, but she didn't care. The sun went down. Cows bawled and Grandpa's milk buckets rattled. Pigs squealed and chickens clamored for food, but Tempe sat. Darkness came.

After a long while Granny walked to the foot of the tree. "If a body had a fight with her best friend, she might forget her chores . . ." Granny's voice trailed off, as if she hoped she wouldn't have to say more. A long pause followed. Tempe was silent. "Maybe she'd mope for a little while, but . . ." Tempe could think of nothing to say. She heard Granny's starched skirts rustle. The voice below changed. It became quite firm. "Tempe, come to supper!"

"Yes'm," said Tempe, and climbed down the tree.

Granny said no more about the quarrel between Tempe and Opal. If she knew from Laurie why the girls quarreled, Tempe never found out.

The next morning she ran over to Opal's house in a panic, afraid Opal would not speak to her. She saw Opal in the yard, and as soon as she was near enough to be heard, Tempe yelled, "I'm sorry!" She was sorry she had brayed like Grandpa's old mule, she told Opal.

"That's all right, Temp." Opal smiled. "I talked ugly, too, but I didn't mean it."

The visit was short. Tempe, feeling restless, trudged home in the heat of the noonday sun. The dazzling sunlight made her dizzy, so she climbed into the Mother Tree and stayed all afternoon.

In the listless days of late summer, Tempe drifted into new habits. She and Opal were friends again, but the feverish, almost-every-day visiting tapered off. While cicadas kept up their ceaseless din in the weeds, while sunflowers and cornstalks parched under the blazing sun, Tempe found refuge in the Mother Tree.

"Don't know why you girls play in the mesquite so much," said Granny. "The live oak's shadier, the chinaberry's cooler."

But the Mother Tree sheltered Tempe and Laurie. After the heat of the day had passed and the blessed south breeze rustled the leafy green lace curtains, Tempe sat among her collected treasures. Laurie listened from her saddle seat below while Tempe sang songs and tapped out rhythms on the delicate cut glass chime.

Tempe grew lax about her chores. Tempe, who could fly around on her slim, almost-eleven legs and do the work quickly, had to be told over and over to water the rosebushes and to carry wood into the kitchen.

One evening, feeling like an angel playing on a harp, Tempe stayed in the tree until darkness fell. At last she straggled to the porch where Granny and Grandpa sat. Granny's voice had an edge on it. "Mighty pretty singing concert you gave us."

Grandpa's voice was sharper. "You forgot your evening chores again."

Tempe's angelic mood refused to shatter. "Yes, sir," she said in a faraway voice. "Tomorrow . . ."

But tomorrow came and it was the same. "I do declare," grumbled Granny, "a big girl like you—you sing, play, forget your duties."

The next morning Granny set Tempe down at the kitchen table and began one of her roundabout talks. Tempe tried to listen, but her mind wandered.

"Will you be glad to get back in your own home?"

Tempe said nothing until she noticed that Granny was staring at her. "Excuse me, what did you say?"

"I said you'll be happy to go home and take care of your father and Phil, won't you?"

It was plain that Granny wanted a "yes" answer. Tempe fidgeted, drumming her fingers on the underside of the table. Happy to go home? No, no, the old house made her unhappy. Philip made her unhappy—well, sometimes, not always. Father? Tempe's thoughts paused, remembering his calm voice, and the strength of his hands, rough and brown like leather. Never, never, in her whole life had Father made her unhappy.

Tempe felt uneasy. Would he and Phil miss her if she didn't go back? They knew how to do everything around the house. Big and strong, both of them, they didn't need her. Father wouldn't care, Tempe told herself, if she stayed here, where she felt contented and safe. She could look after Laurie just as well at Granny's.

Granny was waiting for an answer. Still feeling uneasy, Tempe looked out the window and back again. It would not be the truth to say "yes." On the other hand, she couldn't say "I'm not going." That would be uppity. So she said, "I like it better here," which was the truth.

Granny's face showed she was not satisfied. Tempe stared at her face, thinking, maybe she can read my mind. Maybe she heard me yelling that day in the Mother Tree that I would stay here forever. Or maybe Laurie told her what I said.

Granny stood up. "Get your bonnet and come with me." She called Laurie and took both girls on a tour of the farm. Her voice rambled on, talking to every animal, to every tree, and to every living plant on the place. She pointed this way and that. "Now, I just tell these old bean vines, you *grow*. The sky gives you sunshine and I give you cool water to drink and plenty of poles to run on. So you'd better grow tall!"

On they marched, through the garden and orchard, and back to the windmill. "He's old," she told the girls, "but we treat him good. Your grandpa keeps him patched up and oiled, and he does his job. When the wind blows he goes round and round. He pumps the water that makes the beans grow, and water for the cows and horses and chickens. Everybody and everything work together!"

By now, Tempe knew that this was another of Granny's roundabout lectures. To Laurie it was all fun. "Go, mill," she chanted to the giant wheel spinning high overhead, "round and round!"

Granny's face, usually cheerful, was anxious today. As near as Granny could ever come to preaching, this was it. Usually she just nudged you, a little prod today, another tomorrow. Grandpa said about Granny, "Her thoughts are like chiggers. You don't hear them, or see them, but look out. They sure do itch!"

.This was a real itch, and Granny wouldn't let Tempe dream away each day and evening. She nudged, fretted, and talked until Tempe woke up and began to notice things happening. In Sunday school Tempe found Granny and Opal's mother whispering a secret. Then she noticed whispering at home, and smothered giggles from Laurie.

At the end of the week Granny made her announcement. During supper, she looked around the family group, then grinned straight at Tempe. "This family's going to be busy in the next two weeks. House cleaning, yard cleaning, baking. Tempe's birthday party is only two weeks away!"

A birthday party! Tempe stopped chewing and stared at Granny. Her hand held a spoon, but the hand didn't move. Voices went on around her, but she didn't hear. A birthday party. In all her life nobody had planned a party in her honor. And to think that Granny would do this for her. Granny, displeased with Tempe's careless habits, would do it anyway.

Everybody waited for Tempe to say something. She dropped the spoon and looked down at her plate. Tears welled up. When she could blink them away she smiled. It was a crooked smile to be sure, but a real one. "Thank you, Granny," she said, "thank you."

CHAPTER 12

※

A Brave Girl

TEMPE TRIED VERY HARD TO STOP daydreaming. She would do her chores again, she vowed, and help get ready for the birthday party. She'd be quick and she'd be cheerful. Granny would stop worrying, for her itch would be cured.

Not so. There was the itch about Tempe's health. When she walked into the kitchen wearing one shoe, Granny's eyes grew large. "Put on your other shoe," she said. "Want to scare a body half to death?" Tempe fell asleep on the porch in bright moonlight, and Granny shook her awake. "Want to get moonstruck?"

"I'm not sick, and I'm not moonstruck!"

"Can't be too careful, when a child's about to be eleven years old. Something happens and swoosh—she may not get full grown."

Tempe smiled at Granny's fancy. "What will happen? You think I'll be a midget?"

Granny only looked wise. "Can't ever tell. We have to be careful."

Tempe tried not to throw out hints about birthday

presents, but she looked and listened. She saw Grandpa whittling on something—something small enough to be slipped into his pocket when she came near. She heard Granny and Laurie whispering in the bedroom. Tissue paper rustled, and Laurie crept out, bright-eyed, with one hand over her mouth. She sidled over and leaned on Tempe. "Secret, a secret I'll never tell."

One morning the rural mail carrier delivered another postcard from Father addressed to Tempe. The card read,

> Dear Tempe:
>   Watch for a small package. It is
> for your birthday, from
>   Father and Philip

"Whee!" Tempe squealed, and ran to show the card to the family. Excitement put springs in her legs. Early the next day she bounded down the lane to meet the mail hack. The package did not come, and she plodded back. Each morning new hope set her heart racing, but the days ticked off and there was no package.

Granny had everything planned that last week. She told Tempe about it on Sunday while they cleared off the dinner table. "We'll wash on Monday," she said, "iron the next day, then clean house, and on Thursday you'd better rake the whole yard." At the end of the week, Granny told her, they would bake the birthday cake and color it pink with peppermint candy.

Tempe breathed, "I can't wait." Putting things away in the cupboard, she stopped in the middle of the kitchen with a pickle jar in one hand, a jelly glass in the other, and went into a daydream about the fun she was going to have.

The birthday dinner was to be on Sunday after church services. Opal and her family were invited, of course, and Tempe had asked her second-best school friends, Belle and Judy, who were sisters, and who lived eight miles away, too far to allow weekday visiting. Tempe saw them during the summer only at church and Sunday school. They lived on a ranch, rode cow ponies, went coon hunting at night with their brothers, and were not afraid of snakes, or polecats, or anything.

Granny had an itch about inviting the sisters. "Those girls are awful tomboys," she said, pouring water from the kettle into the dishpan. "Maybe they wouldn't enjoy themselves here."

"Oh, Granny—"

"Can't be too careful."

"You've said that a hundred times. What could happen?"

Granny blinked her eyes and ignored the question. "We'll get all the hard work done ahead of time," she said, washing glassware. "On Sunday, when the company is here, you can sit around all afternoon like a real lady. Won't that be nice?"

"Act like a lady?" Tempe frowned. "That's no fun!"

"No tomboy play, no rough games—"

"Hey, what's a party for?" Tempe wondered what was in Granny's mind. More itches, she decided. Ever since Tempe had said, "I like it better here," Granny's itches had multiplied. She stared into Granny's eyes, getting ready to argue. But what she saw made her turn away. Granny's eyes were not sharp; they did not scold. On her face was an anxious look, the look she had worn the day she took Tempe on a tour of the farm.

Granny murmured, "Can't be too careful . . ."

Tempe wanted more than ever to know what was in her mind. "What could happen?" she asked. "What's a bad sign for a girl's eleventh birthday?"

Granny didn't answer Tempe's straight question. Her anxious look changed to the old wise look. "Bad sign?" She blinked innocently. "Who said anything about a bad sign?"

"Tell me!" Tempe insisted.

Granny pretended hurt feelings. She sighed deeply, fluttered her hands, and hinted that Tempe didn't appreciate help from her poor old granny.

"Oh, my goodness!" Tempe didn't know whether to laugh or cry, but she asked no more questions. She put away the dish towel, slammed the cupboard door and went in search of Grandpa. Catching sight of his straw hat in the peach orchard, she ran to him.

"Granny's got an all-over itch about my birthday. What's bad luck the day a girl turns eleven?"

Grandpa's eyes twinkled. He thought hard, then shook his head. "Sympathize with you, child." He took off his hat to cool his head, then put it on again. "After forty years with your granny, I'm still surprised at new signs and omens."

"She won't admit there *is* an omen."

Grandpa nodded firmly. "I know it well. She drops hints."

"Can't you recollect way back to mountain days?"

"Tell you what I'll do, Tempe," he said thoughtfully, scratching the back of his neck. "I'll look among my memories and see what I can find."

Grandpa found nothing, and the rest of the week went by. Tempe never stopped thinking about the present from Father. Each morning she met the mail hack and each morning was disappointed. On Saturday, the very last day before her birthday, she waited in the dusty road, her throat tight with anxiety. The package just *had* to be here today. Father never went back on a promise, *never*.

The mail carrier handed her a farm paper and an advertisement from Smith Brothers. "Is that all?" Her voice came out raspy. She could feel hot tears spring to her eyelids.

"Yep, that's all." He picked up the reins and clucked at the horse. When he saw Tempe's head droop, he stopped. "What's the matter, little lady, expecting a letter?"

Tempe looked at the ground. He ought to *know*, she

thought, seeing her waiting here every morning. "Package," she mumbled, "birthday."

"By Jingo!" said the mail carrier, "I believe there *was* one, had a dangling label. I said to myself, 'the label's bigger than the package.'"

Tempe took heart while he rummaged in the box beside him, then ran his hand deep in a satchel that hung by the buggy whip.

"By Jerry!" As his big brown hand emerged from the satchel his eyes shone. "Here it is." He held up a large cardboard label from which dangled a brown paper parcel no bigger than a penny matchbox. Tempe's hand shot out. He did not release the parcel. His eyes teased while he squinted at the label. "Is your name Miss Tempe Foster?"

Tempe couldn't stand still. For goodness' sake, he knew her name; he knew everybody's name up and down the mail route. It wasn't funny to joke about a girl's birthday, and it wasn't fair! But she forced herself to be polite. "Yes, sir." When he dropped the parcel in her hand, she clutched it to her heart.

"Giddy-ap!" She heard the mail carrier chuckle as the mail hack plodded up the road. Her lanky legs churned the dust to the house. She burst in, laid the package on the table and danced about, calling the family. They came in a hurry. "See! Little bitty package, it's little, it's precious jewelry, that's what it is!"

"Open it," said Laurie, reaching. "I'll help."

Tempe's fist closed over it, and again she held it to her heart. "First thing in the morning, when I open my eyes, I'll look at it."

She put the package on a chair by her bed. When Laurie showed too much curiosity she hid it under her pillow. All day the thought of precious jewelry warmed her. Was it a ring, a bracelet, a necklace? The puzzle teased her mind and warmed her heart.

On Sunday morning her eyes opened early. Nobody in the house stirred. Beside her Laurie slept, her long eyelashes resting quietly on her round cheeks. Tempe reached for the package and removed the string. From inside the tiny box her trembling fingers drew a gold chain and pendant. They glimmered in the morning light. The pendant, no bigger than a five-cent piece, was shaped like a heart.

To quiet her trembling she let out a deep sigh. How had Father known *exactly* what she wanted? She had seen necklaces in the mail order catalog, but had never *really* thought she would have one, any more than she expected to have a hundred other treasures from those pages. How had Father known? she wondered, then smiled fondly to herself. He had seen her looking and guessed her wish.

She crept from under the quilt, tiptoed to the mirror and held the pendant to her throat, gloating over its beauty. Back in bed, she bent her head to examine the pendant. Why, on one side were hinges! Her thumb

108

pressed the lock, and the cover flew open. A place for a picture.

There was no picture—Father had none—but there was a piece of stiff white paper with writing on it, Father's writing. As a boy Father had learned from a special teacher how to write with curlicues. Tempe squinted at the words. In tiny letters, but with great flourishes, Father had written, in a way to fit the heart-shaped piece of paper.

for
Tempe
a
Brave
Girl

She stared at the words for a long time. For Tempe, a brave girl . . . Once before, Father had said something like that. The night Tempe came down out of the elm tree to feed Laurie because Laurie depended on her, he had said, "It's a brave girl who can change her mind."

An anxious thought nagged her. Would Father think she was brave if he knew she wanted to stay at Granny's, where her work was easy and free of worry?

Strange words, she thought. Change, be brave, change . . . Tempe carefully clicked the lock, then lay back on her pillow and closed her eyes to wait for the day to begin.

CHAPTER 13

Be Sure Your Heart Grows Tall

AT BREAKFAST GRANNY FASTENED THE CHAIN around Tempe's neck, and all morning the gold locket rested gently on her throat.

Her birthday ran in a crazy-quilt pattern. Granny bobbed into her room and took charge of her. "Don't tidy your room, don't make the bed," Tempe was astonished to hear. "You're a lady today, a lady to be waited on."

That was the way it went all day long. Granny was a small shadow who followed Tempe everywhere. She brushed Tempe's long hair and braided it. She took from the closet Tempe's Sunday best dress, the pink organdy, helped her into it and tied the sash. Home again from church, she put away Tempe's dress and brought out second-best clothes for her to wear while playing. The house overflowed with company, but that made no difference. Granny's eyes stayed on Tempe.

The ladies served dinner. Tempe's only duties were to put a plate for Laurie beside her own, and to cut Laurie's food to bite size. "*Two* plates," pleaded Laurie when she sat down, "one for me and one for Sissy." Tempe persuaded Laurie that her imaginary sister would not enjoy sitting at the table among strangers.

After dinner the girls gathered in Tempe's room to admire the locket and her other presents. There was a satin pincushion from Granny and Laurie, a wooden pintray carved by Grandpa, a jump rope from Opal, and two stiff, rustling hair ribbons from Belle and Judy. The girls were hardly settled when Granny bustled in and shooed them out of the house to play.

The older folks sat on the shady porch, rocking and swishing paper fans. Party or no party, Grandpa had stretched out on the porch cot to take his afternoon rest. Laurie was busy with Opal's little brothers. She allowed the boys a turn at her saddle seat in the mesquite tree, whereupon they turned into war-whooping Indians. When Tempe's group plunged into a wild game of hide-and-seek the younger children climbed out of the tree and joined them. At Tempe's turn to hide she ran to the porch and crouched behind Grandpa's cot. Granny dropped her fan and stood up.

"You younguns!" she shouted in a voice Tempe didn't recognize. "Stay off the porch, stay out of the house!"

Tempe had never seen Granny so alarmed. She wasn't acting like herself at all, and the visitors were surprised. In whispers Tempe told Opal and Belle and Judy about Granny's itch, and it became a tantalizing mystery. By sundown when all the company left, nobody had learned

Granny's reason for following Tempe about on her eleventh birthday.

That evening Granny shooed Tempe off to bed early and insisted on tucking her and Laurie in. She looked tired. Usually her hair was coiled into a smooth white bun high on her head. Tonight wisps of hair straggled, and a hairpin fell on the covers of Tempe's bed.

"My birthday has worked you to death," said Tempe, smiling. "Aren't you going to tell me the secret?"

Once more Granny played innocent. She said sharply that Tempe had better watch out, eleven-year-olds weren't too big to spank.

Chuckling to herself, Tempe went to sleep. When she opened her eyes, sunlight streamed in through the windows, and there sat Granny in the bedroom rocker. She wore her ruffled pink apron, and her hair was in its usual neat bun. She was smiling like an angel.

"You're through the vale of shadow." Granny was very pleased with herself. "From this day forward, you will get full-grown."

Tempe stretched and yawned. It was fun to be eleven years old, but the mystery again plagued her. "What was your worry, yesterday?"

Granny blinked and went on talking. "From now on, you'll carry your share without complaining."

"But, Granny—"

"Going to make your father happy."

Tempe flounced out of bed, impatient with the turn of

the conversation. She was going to stop chasing Granny's quicksilver thoughts, she decided. Granny was two persons in one. There was Granny who listened with her heart and spoke in a mysterious language; then there was Granny who kept turning back to her roundabout lecture.

After breakfast Tempe went to the barn to feed the pigs and chickens. Grandpa followed her. Out of Granny's hearing he crooked his finger. "She gave you a hard run yesterday," he said.

Tempe forgot the vow to put Granny's notions out of her mind. "She's happy today." She grinned at Grandpa. "The thing she feared didn't happen."

He chuckled. "Last night it came to me."

Tempe set down the feed bucket. "What came to you?"

"I recollected way back when your father was eleven years old."

"Tell me!" She shook his arm. "Did she have an itch about him?"

Grandpa nodded. "That she did. All day long, followed him about."

"What did she fear?"

"Back in mountain country, some folks believe if a child on his eleventh birthday looks under a bed, he won't get full-grown."

Tempe burst out laughing. "So that's why she handed me my shoes, why she wouldn't let me sweep the floor or hide behind your cot." Weak from laughing, she leaned on a fence post. "A big girl like me, healthy as a yearling calf, tall for my age, and Granny worries about me being a midget. Just imagine!"

Grandpa smiled, then his face grew serious. He sat on a log and lighted his pipe, motioning for Tempe to sit beside him. "Your granny is full of fancies. We smile at her, and sometimes we forget that she is very wise."

"Oh, yes—"

"She isn't one that preaches. She nudges you and pushes you in the right direction. If you listen close and read her heart, you know . . ."

Tempe waited.

"Your body will grow," he said, "of that your granny is sure." Tempe looked up quickly. "But she wants to be sure your heart grows tall."

Tempe said "Oh" and thought about it. She nodded. "I see." She thought about it all that day, and the next and the next.

CHAPTER 14

Rock Me to Sleep

TODAY WAS IRONING DAY. Granny had done the fancy starched pieces and the ruffly pieces. Now Tempe, in the kitchen, was finishing the easy flat work. The slow, steady work gave her time to think. Wearing the new locket, she was remembering with joy her birthday party and Father's gift. He was the best father in the world, she thought.

With her heart filled with love she slipped back into her habit of daydreaming. Swish, swish, went the iron over the ironing board. She stood on her left foot and kept time with the swish of the iron by sweeping her right foot back and forth over the kitchen floor. If it made her happy to stay at Granny's, she told herself, Father would consent.

Granny broke into her dream with a reminder. "The menfolks will be home next week. We must go over to your house and clean it up."

Tempe's heart began to chill. She thought of the cold bare floors in Father's house on winter mornings. She thought of trying to part her own hair in a straight line

116

and braid it, and of searching for Laurie's stockings, lost in a mountain of bedcovers. She thought of smoky lamp chimneys and wet wood that wouldn't burn, the dinners to be cooked and no one else to watch Laurie.

Tempe groaned. She just couldn't return home to live. Where would she keep her new treasures now displayed in the Mother Tree? Philip's stinging words came back to her. "Trash—keep them at the barn!"

The next day Grandpa hitched the team to the wagon, and they all set out along the dusty road. Tempe and Laurie sat on the floor of the wagon bed. With the tail gate down they swung their feet clear and jogged along looking backward. Laurie clutched Butterflake and Rags in her arms. Tempe was good-natured until Laurie moved close to her, explaining, "I have to leave room for Sissy on the other side."

"Don't crowd me!" snapped Tempe, who was tired of Sissy, the imaginary sister, and tired of Laurie's wriggling.

As the wagon turned off the road, Tempe glanced over her shoulder at her home. It looked shabby and forlorn. She quickly turned her head away.

When the wagon stopped they all piled out. Granny said, "Little old house looks lonesome, but all it needs is folks around again."

Inside they found the rooms hot and stifling. Panting for cool air, Tempe opened the doors wide and threw up groaning windows. The groans echoed against the walls of the empty house. Tempe brushed by the empty chair that sat in front of the cold fireplace and set it in motion. The chair rocked and squeaked all by itself. Tempe couldn't bear to look. It made her think of Mother's singing, and of the fever, quick and cruel, that had taken her away.

Tempe wanted to run out of the house, but she couldn't. She had to stay and help Granny with the cleaning.

Laurie was quiet today, sticking close to Tempe. She ignored a plea to "go outside and play." Solemn of face, dragging a doll from each hand, she trailed Tempe from room to room.

Granny must have read the feelings of Tempe and Laurie, for she asked in a hearty voice, "You girls want to sing a song while we work?" Tempe could not find her voice. Laurie, who usually brightened to match Granny's moods, did not reply. Granny said no more.

Sweeping the bedroom, Tempe came upon a pair of Philip's socks, and was reminded of his rude laugh. In the sitting room the sagging curtain brought back the day Phil had pulled the covers from her bed. The memory made her angry all over again.

The old black range—a friend on cold winter mornings—was not a friend today. Boil the beans, boil the beans. Don't forget the baking powder or the bread won't rise . . . To escape her bad dream Tempe slipped into a good dream.

Never mind, never mind, she told herself. She would

be living at Granny's.

"Temp-ee! Where are you?" From the sound of Granny's voice, she must have called several times. Tempe hurried into the bedroom. "I've been thinking. Why couldn't you and Laurie have this room? Put your double bed in the corner. There's room in the closet for all your clothes."

"But," said Tempe, "it belongs to the menfolks."

"Maybe I'll speak to your father," said Granny thoughtfully. "He and Phil could put their cots on the porch or in the middle room." Tempe's eyes widened. "I mean until the lean-to is finished."

"When will it be finished?"

"Won't take long. They'll bring home money to buy lumber and shingles and nails. Your grandpa will help. Should be finished before winter comes."

The thought of a bedroom of her own did not lure Tempe back to Father's house. She longed to return to Granny's house, with its homey smells and homey feeling. She wanted to quench her thirst with a long cool drink and crawl into the Mother Tree. She would go behind the green leaf curtains, lie down, and in the summer dusk listen to the comforting sounds of the night—the rustling of tree limbs and the sing-song of the crickets.

When the work at Father's house was finished they closed the doors and in the wagon rattled down the lane toward home. Home, her home, Tempe thought dreamily.

After chores were done and supper was over, the Mother Tree beckoned to her. She climbed to the tree house. The night coolness bathed her arms, her neck, and her legs. Here in her lofty retreat, with the stars blinking down, was peace. Here was freedom. She would never, never, leave.

From somewhere she heard Laurie's quavering voice. "Temp-ee." The voice called and called. Tempe would not answer. The voice came closer. Afraid of the dark, afraid of being alone, Laurie whimpered from the foot of the tree, "Where are you?"

Tempe kept very still. Laurie began to climb; her fumbling steps set tree limbs swaying. Groaning and panting, she almost wept. But as her warm body sank down beside Tempe, Laurie gave a glad cry. "You didn't answer, but I found you!"

"Sh-h-h," said Tempe. Laurie settled down. The noises of the night ceased, and all was still. The girls were almost asleep when they heard Granny's voice. When it was time for bed, Granny sometimes called Laurie with an old sleepy time song. If Laurie did not answer the first verse, or if Tempe did not lead her into the house, Granny would go to the second verse and to the third and fourth, singing louder all the time. From the kitchen Granny began,

*"Hush little baby, don't say a word
Mama's gonna buy you a mockingbird."*

Tempe could not move. Her thoughts drifted on. Wait, wait. The night was enchanted. Please, please, her mind cried, let nothing break its spell. Let Laurie feel the magic and find her way to bed alone.

A soft voice came from beside her, a sleepy voice. "I found you—rock me to sleep, Mother."

Mother! The word jerked Tempe rudely awake. Her heart pounded as she strained to hear Laurie's pleading words. "Rock me to sleep. The elves hid you away, but I found you—in the Mother Tree."

CHAPTER 15

❧

Long Live the Pioneers

THE NEXT MORNING TEMPE WOKE EARLY, left Laurie asleep, and walked through her outside chores, shaken and bewildered. Nothing seemed real, after what had happened last night. Hearing Laurie say, "Rock me to sleep, Mother," had alarmed her. She could not remember climbing down from the tree and going to bed.

Tempe had promised Father to "keep an eye on Laurie" and to give him a report when he came home. Since Father left, Laurie had asked no questions about Mother, and that meant good news—until last night. Now, if Laurie really believed that their mother was hidden in the Mother Tree, Tempe would have bad news to tell.

As she poured drinking water for the chickens, Tempe thought it all over again. Last night in the warm black dusk, she had been sure that Laurie believed what she said about Mother and the elves. But now the shadows were gone, and the sun was shining. Daytime was the time to believe in real things. This morning Tempe wanted to believe that Laurie had called out to Mother in a dream, a dream easily forgotten. But she was not sure. Would Laurie, in the daytime, forget her unreal fancies? Tempe did not know, and the question made her restless and uneasy. She wished she could tell Father about it now. But Father was far away.

Grandpa had extra duties for Tempe, and she was glad to keep her hands busy. It was peach-drying season. Every year the Foster family dried extra peaches and saved them to eat during the fall and winter. Today was "turning day." Somebody must climb to the roof of the front porch where the peaches were drying and turn over every peach half, exposing it to the fierce heat of the Texas sun.

Grandpa said, "Tempe, you're surefooted and agile. Would you like to play monkey and do the climbing?"

Tempe did not mind. It was tedious work to turn hundreds of peach halves, but she liked to climb high and see far off. Wearing a skimpy, faded dress she squatted on the roof and worked, scarcely knowing what she did, for she could not keep her mind away from Laurie and Laurie's unreal world. Was it only a way of playing? Or did Laurie cling to the Mother Tree in the way she once clung to Mother?

If this were true, leaving the Mother Tree would bring great sorrow to Laurie. Tempe wished she knew Laurie's real feelings. Climbing down the ladder, she wished again that Father were here to help her sort out the truth.

Granny asked her to walk down the lane to the mailbox. When she opened the box and found two letters from Father, one addressed to "Miss Tempe Foster," a feeling of great relief washed over her. A message from Father, just what she needed.

She sat on a rock beside the lane and tore open the envelope. The letter said the men had finished threshing the grain and were packing to start home. It had been hard work, Father said, but they had earned enough money to build the lean-to on the house.

The old house. Tempe didn't want to think about it. The letter told what the family would soon be doing. "Play time is over for you girls, and work begins again," Father wrote. "If you are like me, it isn't the work that hurts, it's the worry."

The words sounded like Father, but without the warmth of his voice, they were a lecture. Tempe's heart dragged. Before she slipped the letter back into the envelope she read once more the last lines. "We'll all work and worry together. Your loving Father."

Tempe rose and shuffled her way toward the house, suddenly very tired. She was tired of thinking about the old house and Laurie, and tired of being confused. At the back gate she remembered Opal. Dear Opal, a good listener and a good friend. By the time she had put the letters in Granny's hand, her mind was alive with a plan. She gazed earnestly into Granny's face and asked for a day away from home, a day away from Laurie.

Granny turned to Grandpa, who nodded. "Our girl

worked mighty hard turning peaches."

Granny put her hand under Tempe's chin. "Don't look so pitiful, child. It's all right. Run along."

Tempe set out quickly through the pasture, full of thoughts she would spill out to Opal. Words still rang in her mind—Father's words, "play time is over," and Laurie's words, "rock me to sleep, Mother."

She arrived at Opal's flushed from walking fast in the heat, and in a nervous hurry to talk. She led Opal to the shade of the oak tree where they could be alone.

"I don't know what to do!" she said, pacing about under the tree, kicking at fallen leaves, "We have to leave Granny's, and Laurie's heart will break—"

"Maybe she's only pretending."

"And maybe she's not!"

Opal looked anxiously at her. "Why don't you sit down?"

Tempe sat flat on the ground, but her feet were restless. Her ankles twisted, while one hand twisted her braided hair. "Oh, I'm so mixed up! It's all too spooky for me to understand!"

Sympathizing, Opal nodded. "Did you tell your grandpa?"

Tempe was astonished. "Goodness no! He and Granny don't know anything about Laurie's—"

"Are you sure?"

Nothing was solved, but the telling calmed Tempe. Opal went to the house and brought back two glasses of lemonade. After drinking lemonade Tempe was able to think of other things. She listened to Opal's ideas. Would Tempe like to play hopscotch, or to swing from the rafters of the hayloft? Tempe chose the hayloft, but while they walked toward it, Opal had a third idea, which was the best idea of all. "Why don't we go exploring? Bleached bones!"

Tempe stared at her. "What do you mean, bleached bones?"

"Don't you remember—the cow skeleton?"

Then Tempe remembered. Somewhere up the creek were the bones of an animal that had died years before. Opal's father had told her about it. Long seasons of sun and rain and wind had taken away everything but white bones, gleaming in the sun. "Let's go!" said Tempe. A bleached bone collection! That would be as elegant as a stuffed deer head over the mantel.

Opal's mother agreed that an exploring trip was fine. The girls set out with sacks slung over their shoulders. On the way they were tempted by beautiful rocks and cactus, but decided to save room in their sacks for bones. Half an hour later, from far off, they saw the skeleton's ribs shining white. They began to run. There, in a sunny, dry spot was the head, a beautiful bleached skull with staring, empty eye sockets, brittle jaw bones and teeth.

The girls stared. "Maybe it was an ox," said Opal, "hauling an oxcart, bringing the brave pioneers."

"Yes," breathed Tempe, her mind taking wings. How

many summers and winters had come and gone, how many blizzards and hailstorms had tormented the lonely land since those brave souls had searched in vain for water and shelter? "Maybe the driver staggered away to safety," said Tempe, with wide, sweeping gestures, "leaving the poor, helpless ox to his death."

"Yeah," agreed Opal.

Both girls knew it was a farmer's cow—it might have died with the heaves—but the pioneer story was braver.

Opal bent her knees and lovingly lifted the bleached skull. "Let's hang it in the Mother Tree."

They took the choice pieces—the long gleaming ribs, of course, and the shank bones. They left the mummified feet and the rest of the skeleton to the sun and the rain and the wind.

On the way back the giant idea struck their minds. It began when Tempe shouldered her heavy sack, strode across the prairie and shouted, "Long live the pioneers!"

"There ought to be a monument," said Opal.

Tempe stared into her eyes. "You mean build a monument?"

"Why not?"

"Here on the prairie? Who would ever see it?"

"That's so," admitted Opal. "We could build it at your place."

Tempe's imagination flamed. "In the Mother Tree!"

Opal got permission from her mother, and off they went. The sacks bounced on their backs as they galloped toward Granny's. They toiled for hours. To make room for the monument in the tree, they took from the platform everything but rocks. Down came the precious cut glass chime, the snakeskin, arrowheads, cactus, and bird's nest. Left were the volcanic rocks, the shiny black rock, earth-colored rocks and the rocks that looked like granite. The pipe bell was left hanging overhead, out of the way.

Laurie wanted to help, so they took her with them on a short rock hunt. They needed flat stones for the monument's foundation, and found them out past the peach orchard, big ones. Under their weight Tempe and Opal staggered back to the tree. Hauling the stones up the sloping tree trunk and higher to the platform took all their strength. With the flat stones as a base they stacked rocks in pyramid fashion, layer on layer, with small ones tapering to a dramatic point.

Granny strolled by. "Are you going to overload that limb?"

"No, ma'am," said Opal.

"No, Granny," said Tempe. The girls thought they were speaking true.

"What on earth *is* it?" Granny squinted upward.

The girls, sweating and panting, paused and stood beside their creation. "It's a monument," Opal said with pride.

"A monument to the pioneers," said Tempe.

"My, my," said Granny, shaking her head. "You be careful, now hear? Don't make it any bigger, it's heavy enough."

"Yes, ma'am," said the girls in an absent-minded way, for they were not worried. What if the limb sagged a bit? What if the tree house, with its giant load, dipped lower with each armload of rocks? When the pyramid was finished, they arranged the gleaming rib bones and shank bones along its sloping surface. The skull with empty eye sockets and shining white teeth crowned the peak of the monument.

They crawled down and looked at it from the yard, backing off a few steps, then walking backward, past the rosebushes, past the chinaberry tree as far as the yard gate. "It looks beautiful from far away," said Tempe. Opal agreed. They crawled back to their perch. There was just room enough to stand, with Tempe on the right and Opal on the left. Tempe clanged the pipe bell. Opal felt moved to recite a poem. It was a peach of a poem; it had fifteen verses, and Opal remembered every line.

Tempe couldn't remember any poems, but her voice rang out, "Long live the pioneers!" Clang, clang.

In the middle of the afternoon the wind turned cool and whistled around the house. It rustled dried weeds, rolled them into balls and pushed them down the lane. Granny, alert to changes in the weather, came out and scanned the sky. "Feels stormy," she said. "See those dark clouds?"

The clouds were small against the horizon. They did not look scary to Tempe. But when the sun disappeared and the sky darkened, Granny turned to Opal. "We love

to have you visit us, but your folks will be worried. Might
rain. You'd better scoot home early today."

Opal found her bonnet and told them all good-bye.
Tempe went with her as far as the pasture gate. "Long
live the pioneers!" she called out as Opal walked away.

CHAPTER 16

The Storm

AS DARK CLOUDS PILED UP IN THE SKY it seemed more like night than day. The howling wind drove Tempe inside. From the kitchen window she watched the wind play its savage tricks.

It attacked the windmill tower and left it swaying. It snapped cornstalks in half and lopped off yellow heads of sunflowers. In its path sturdy trees trembled.

As daylight dwindled Tempe ventured outside with Grandpa to look after the livestock. The wind punished her, turning her skirt inside out and whipping sand in her face.

She shooed all the chickens inside the hen house and bolted the door. After Grandpa milked the cows Tempe helped him drive all the uneasy farm animals into shelters. He said to Tempe, "Don't worry. They will ride it out."

The screaming wind pushed Tempe and Grandpa across the yard to the house. As they struggled to open the back door a tin washtub fell from its hanging place on the porch and rolled into the yard. "We've got a real blow tonight," he shouted, running after the tub. Inside, he said to Granny, "After supper we'll bring in the wash-tubs and the porch chairs."

"Don't forget your cot," said Granny.

When Tempe sat down, Laurie came close and leaned against her shoulder.

Grandpa looked out the window. "We may lose some shingles from the roof. Trees out there are dancing a jig."

Granny said, "Let her blow. You've done all that can be done." She gazed into the anxious faces of the girls. "Little old house will shelter us all. Now, let's have supper." So the family sat down and tried to ignore the attacking wind.

The girls went to bed. Laurie fell asleep right away. Tempe could feel the house shudder in the wind. Even their bed trembled a little. Before she drifted off she listened to voices in the parlor.

Granny's was filled with worry. "They're on the road tonight—no roof over their heads."

Tempe's heart twisted. Father and Philip were somewhere out there, battling the cruel wind.

"They'll be all right," said Grandpa.

"But I've heard of travelers—real trouble—"

Grandpa's voice was calm. "They'll find a wagon yard, or some safe place."

Tempe relaxed, feeling Grandpa's confidence. Father always knew the wise thing to do. The voices came again, but with less worry.

"—still a-blowing."

"—trees a-dancing."

Trees dancing. Tempe was sure that Grandpa meant the spindling chinaberry, or the peach trees beyond the garden. He couldn't mean sturdy old trees that had outlived many windstorms and blizzards, trees that had stood firm since Father was a boy—the spreading live oak and the old mesquite. The Mother Tree was too strong for the wind, too tough and old. Its roots went down, down, deep into the earth. Lashed by the wind, it would hug the earth and hang on.

Wailing like sad music, the wind brought weird dreams to Tempe. Long after the house was dark and sleeping, she thought she heard a giant prowling, trying to push the house over with one hand. She thought she saw his hairy paw cover the window.

She heard a squeaking, and there was her mother's chair, rocking by itself; its squeaking filled her ears. Sitting up, she heard nothing but the wind. Foolish, foolish, she told herself, and lay back on the pillow.

Later in the night groaning sounds brought her wide awake. She sat up and listened. No one in the house stirred. Above the moan of thunder, the sound came again.

Her bare feet tiptoed through the house. She was afraid, not of the giant, for that was a dream, but afraid to know about the groaning. Yet she had to know. Tree limbs squeak, she thought with dread, and tree trunks groan . . .

At the kitchen window she could see nothing but blackness outside. The back door was a live thing in her hand; it leaped away from her. Careful, careful; if Grandpa heard her he would keep her inside the house. On the porch her nightgown flew about her head. She needed all her strength to push the door shut.

The groaning was louder. Jagged lightning showed her the tree house, with its rocks and bones gleaming white. The wind was beating the tree without mercy. The right wing heaved up and down. The left wing, burdened with the rock monument, floundered. With every lash of the wind it gave out a helpless groan.

"Don't hurt the tree!" she pleaded. The wind tore loose two shank bones from the monument and sent them flying. It wrenched Laurie's saddle from the tree fork and flung it against the fence. "Don't break Laurie's heart!"

The wind hurled the splint basket that held Laurie's elves. Tempe ducked, and a rock whistled by her ear.

The wind trounced the left wing of the tree; the tree trembled, bringing down a stream of rocks. "Go away!" said Tempe in anger. The tree house dipped dangerously. Tempe danced about, shaking her fist. "That's mine!" she shouted. "That's my tree. Leave it alone!"

White bones rolled to the ground. The gleaming skull landed at her feet. "You're cruel!" she screamed at the wind. "You're cruel, and I hate you!"

She was crying now, but above the storm she heard another voice. She turned to see Laurie running toward her, with nightgown billowing. She grasped Laurie and turned her around. "Back! Go back in the house!"

"No!" Laurie threw her arms around Tempe's waist. "No!"

"How did you get the door open?"

"The wind took it—"

Tempe shook off Laurie's grasp and bounded up the porch steps. The wind was roaring into the kitchen. Any moment she would see lamplight in the house. With all her weight against the door she closed it.

Back in the yard she heard a crackling sound.

Laurie screamed at the wind, "You're bad, bad, bad!"

A splintering sound roared in Tempe's ears. She grabbed Laurie and backed away. The left wing of the mesquite broke away and crashed to the earth, spilling the tree house with its load of rocks and bones, guy wires and iron pipe.

Seeing the raw, white gash in the wounded tree, Tempe burst into tears. When no more treasures flew through the air, she moved toward the Mother Tree. She sank to its base, her strength gone. The wind—quick and cruel— had taken everything.

"Don't cry, Tempe." Laurie stroked her cheek and nestled close. Laurie was the comforter now. "Never mind, Tempe, never mind."

It had begun to rain. The rain stung their faces, wet their hair to the scalp, and plastered nightgowns to their skin. Tempe hardly noticed. She was as wet as she could get, and she had cried all her tears.

After a while the wind, as if resting from its giant task, began to change. Its insults weakened to shouts, then shouts weakened to moans. Tempe leaned against the tree trunk and felt the pelting rain grow gentler.

There was something strange about Laurie, she thought. Laurie was not sad. She had not wept during the storm. The wind had destroyed the Mother Tree before her eyes, and she had not shed a tear. Maybe she didn't understand.

Tempe told her, "The storm took away all your toys." Laurie showed no concern. "Your pooka is lost."

"Pooka's lost," said Laurie.

"Your elves are lost."

Laurie turned to face Tempe. "Mean old elves! They're gone." Tempe could not understand. Laurie said in an angry voice, "Elves are bad. Boogers are bad. They're all dead and gone."

To be sure that Laurie understood Tempe told her, "The Mother Tree—" Her own voice almost broke. "It's gone."

Laurie hummed a little tune. She put her arms around Tempe and chanted a sort of song. "Elves are dead and gone, and I am glad."

A lost feeling stole over Tempe. Why was Laurie glad?

Laurie kept up her sing-song. "The Mother Tree is dead and gone, and I am glad."

It was then that Tempe knew she had been wrong

about Laurie's need. Laurie had a real need, but it was not for the Mother Tree. Tempe held her close, thinking, Laurie needs *me*. Whatever I am, the way I am, Laurie needs me.

The girls didn't notice lamplight in the house. They saw no light at all until Grandpa's lantern shone in their faces. He led them into the kitchen. Granny was ready with towels and dry nightgowns. There was no scolding, only sympathy for Tempe and Laurie.

Granny rubbed their hair almost dry. "Wash your feet," she said, "then back to bed. You can take all-over baths tomorrow."

"No," said Laurie. "The storm scrubbed me. I'm clean."

Tempe nodded agreement.

Grandpa peered out the window. "The storm is about over."

Laurie said, "Tempe told the wind to stop, and it did." She clasped Tempe's hand. "Tempe is stronger than the wind."

The girls went to bed, but Tempe's mind kept turning. Laurie thinks I'm strong . . . am I? Am I stronger than the storm that took away the Mother Tree? Laurie thinks I am. Am I stronger than the fever that took Mother? Laurie would think so. Laurie depends on me. Maybe I *am* strong. Maybe I'm stronger than I know.

Laurie's excitement was slow to drain away. She chattered to Tempe, who didn't listen. She murmured to her dolls, "Go to sleep, sleep." Tempe thought she had drifted off, but in the quiet room came her voice, slow and steady, "Temp-ee . . ." When Tempe didn't answer she began again. "Temp-ee . . ."

With a start Tempe remembered Laurie's old question about Mother, the question Tempe and Father had come to dread. Laurie always began her question in just this way. Tempe sat up and held her breath.

The voice came again. "Temp-ee . . ."

"Yes?"

"When is Father coming home?"

Relief washed over Tempe. Relief and delight. She let out her breath, lay down and patted Laurie's hand. "Tomorrow, we hope."

Laurie had changed, she thought; as Father had said, a four-year-old changes fast. Laurie's sad, brooding thoughts about Mother were gone. How pleased Father would be! She could imagine his smile—not his slow smile, but a quick, happy smile of surprise. Tempe could hardly wait to see it.

A new thought came to Tempe. In a dazed way she wondered if she, too, had changed. The thought was fuzzy, and she didn't understand why it had come to her mind. She'd tell Father about it when he came home. Maybe he could explain.

CHAPTER 17

❧

Homecoming Day

THE NEXT DAY WAS SUNNY AND MILD. When Grandpa came back from the barn he looked cheerful. During the storm, he said, not a hair was harmed among the livestock; not a feather was blown off the flock. Many shingles were missing from the roof of the house, but with the men due home soon, the repair job would be easy.

Granny warmed to Grandpa's cheery words. She put on her fanciest apron and planned chicken and dumplings for dinner. "This is homecoming day!" she said. "I feel it in my bones."

Tempe dreaded to leave the house. She didn't want to see the back yard; she didn't want to look at the broken tree. But the tree beckoned.

The splintered-off left wing sprawled on the ground, but at the fork of the tree, a few slivers of wood had not broken away. The left wing clung to the tree by a thread. Its shattered trunk, naked of bark and sharp as a dagger, pointed to the sky. Tree branches littered the yard in wild confusion. The old door, torn from its place by the wind and dropped, leaned at a crazy angle against the fence. Tempe's eyes filled with tears.

Grandpa came into the yard carrying a rake, a saw, and an ax. Tempe looked quickly toward the tree and shuddered. The ax would level the tree to the ground, and there would be nothing left for her to remember.

When Grandpa began stacking broken tree branches she made an effort to help. "Good girl," he said. "Didn't think you'd feel like cleaning up."

It was true, she did not feel like working, but she kept busy. Her eyes were busy, searching among the litter for her treasures. She wanted to find a keepsake, one treasure to help her remember the Mother Tree. She found broken bones, but they were not beautiful any more. Where was the joint of pipe that had rung like a bell in the tree? She could not find it.

She and Grandpa piled trash and rocks in a corner of the yard. They did not touch the crippled tree. The left wing sprawled on the ground just as they had found it.

Grandpa walked to the tree and looked it over thoughtfully. When he picked up his ax Tempe ran to her room and covered her ears with her hands. The blows of the ax rang out. Her hands could not shut out the sound. She heard the grunt of Grandpa's saw, then more chopping. Would he leave a stump or cut off the tree level with the ground? Either way, the empty place would be a painful thing to see.

Sounds from the yard stopped, and there was a long silence. Tempe grew restless in her room. Granny and

Laurie were busy in the kitchen, but she did not feel like joining them. Her mind kept turning toward the tree. Presently Grandpa called from outside. "Tempe! Come look!"

Her steps were slow. Her eyes saw only the ground. She heard Grandpa ask proudly, "There, doesn't it look better?"

She raised her eyes. The unspoiled half of the mesquite tree stood before her. Fronds of green lace swayed and shimmered in a light breeze. She gasped, "I thought—"

"A strong old tree," he said. "It will live."

He had sawed off the broken left wing, hauled it away and raked the ground clean. The smell of creosote was in the air, for he had painted the raw, white wound. The scar was stained a dark brown.

"After a time," he told her, "as the tree grows, you won't notice the scar."

She let out her breath. "It's beautiful."

Then she gazed at the blank space where the left wing of the tree had swayed and shimmered. Gone, she thought . . . all gone. In the place where she had worked and played all summer there was nothing. The beauty of the living tree filled her eyes, but doubts came to her mind. The Mother Tree and her summer of joy— were they blanked out forever?

No, no, her heart answered. They were with her still, in memory. Her summer refuge—the tree that adopted

Tempe and Laurie until they were strong enough to go along without Mother—was with her still, in memory. She could not forget the tree any more than she could forget Mother.

Grandpa brought something to her. "I found this," he said, "still tied to the limb."

The pipe bell. "Oh, thank you." Tempe cradled it in her hands. This would be her keepsake. She knew just the right place to hang it. Father would help her tie it on a high limb of the elm tree in her own back yard, at home.

Home? Her thoughts stopped short. What place did she call home? Then she knew. Home is where a person belongs, she thought. For a time this summer, I belonged in the Mother Tree. I needed the tree. But it's better to need your own folks and to have your own folks need you.

She cleaned the pipe bell and took it to her room. After Father and Phil arrived, she would pack it with her things and get them ready for the trip home in Father's wagon.

Tempe's heart was warm with the feeling that Father would soon be here. He was just around the bend of the road, or the next bend, or the next. She had so much to tell him. "Keep an eye on Laurie," he had said, "and tell me when I get back." Now she would keep her promise.

Tempe changed her clothes and put on her new red hair ribbon. She helped Laurie into a starchy clean dress and tried to keep her away from dirt. Laurie swung on the gate for hours, calling out every time she heard a strange sound. "Here they come, there they are. It's Father—"

The day wore on. In the middle of the afternoon the Fosters, worn out by false alarms, did not hear the sound of horses' feet until they were almost at the gate.

The clopity-clop was a slow, tired sound. The team, glistening with sweat, jogged to a tired halt. Even the dusty wagon, with the load of lumber sagging at the back, looked tired.

By the time Father had braked the wheel and wound the lines around the brake handle, Tempe had helped Laurie climb to the spring seat of the wagon. As Laurie smothered Father and Philip with hugs and moist kisses, their dusty faces broke into wide grins.

At the table, between bites of chicken, the men told stories of their travels. "Where did you stay last night in the storm?" asked Granny.

Father smiled. "I knew you would worry. A farmer put us up. Let us drive the wagon right into his big hay barn."

"Luck—pure luck," said Phil, with his mouth full.

When Father announced with pride, "Phil learned to cook this summer," Tempe felt a twinge of her old resentment.

But Phil didn't wear his old smug look. Taller and browner than she remembered, he turned to Tempe and said quite seriously, "I missed your good old beans, Temp. What do you put in them to make them taste good?"

Surprised, Tempe could say nothing. Later, when the family gathered on the back porch, Phil went to the wagon and returned carrying a bucket heavy with souvenirs. Half-embarrassed, he put it at Tempe's feet. "For your collection," he said.

When she saw what lay on top, Tempe squealed, "Arrowheads! And they're perfect. Oh, Phil!"

From the collection came rocks as red as cinnamon and rocks spotted like a pinto pony. There was a gleaming, polished lump that she could almost see through. "Is it made of glass? It's as big as my fist!"

"Crystal," said Phil, his eyes proud and gleaming, "from a cave in Arkansas—or that's what the fellow said. I traded for it."

Tempe sprang up to give Phil a big hug. Before she remembered that he wouldn't like it, she had done it. Phil did not pull away. He was pleased.

Tempe displayed her new treasures along the edge of the porch and sat down on the steps to stare at the array. The family crowded around to see Phil's gifts, then scattered again. Laurie did not calm down all afternoon. She whirled from Father to Philip and back again, ignoring everyone else. Tempe gave up urging her to take an afternoon nap. She could hear Laurie's piping voice in a corner of the yard, pouring out a long recital to Father. He came to Tempe and dropped beside her.

"What is this about the tree that's dead and gone? Laurie calls it the Mother Tree."

"Oh, Father"—she turned her face toward him—"I have so much to tell you, it will take all day."

He glanced toward the afternoon sun and said in a half-joking tone, "In that case, you'd better begin now."

And she did. She began with, "While you were gone, Laurie changed." Tempe told him, "Last night she asked, 'When is *Father* coming home?'"

The news brought out his sudden wide smile, just as she had expected. When he put an arm around Tempe and drew her close, she thought her heart would burst.

"I'm glad," said Father, "and I'd like to hear all about it."

She thought she told him everything. But weeks later, after the lean-to had been built and the old house seemed like a new house, after Tempe had a room of her own—well, almost, for Laurie was with her—she would remember something and begin, "Last summer, at Granny's . . ."

With the telling of it her sorrow fell away, and Tempe remembered only the happy times that had come to her in the Mother Tree.

Sources of Folk Songs

THE FOLK SONGS MENTIONED in *The Mother Tree* may be found in many collections. Here is where I saw them:

1. *American Ballads and Folk Songs*
   John A. and Alan Lomax
   Macmillan Company, New York, 1934

   "Shoot the Buffalo"

2. *Our Singing Country,* a Second Volume of American Ballads and Folk Songs
   John A. and Alan Lomax
   Macmillan Company, New York, 1941

   "Hush Li'l Baby"
   "Married Me a Wife"

3. *The Folk Songs of North America in the English Language*
   Alan Lomax
   Doubleday & Company, Garden City, New York, 1960

   "Green Grows the Laurel"